FLAMING ARROWS

by William O. Steele

Flaming Arrows

WILLIAM O. STEELE

Illustrated by Paul Galdone

A VOYAGER BOOK
Harcourt Brace Jovanovich, Inc., New York

A B C D E F G H I J

ISBN 0-15-631550-5

Library of Congress Catalog Card Number: 57-6791

Printed in the United States of America

For Margaret

*For love, and for never
changing so much as a
comma without asking*

FLAMING ARROWS

Chapter One

"I reckon it's suppertime," remarked Chad, letting his ax slip to the ground. He straightened up slowly. He was bone-tired, and his back was one fierce ache. But he was proud of himself. He figured he'd never worked so hard before in all his eleven years, for he'd spent this livelong day chopping trees and had done a man's work.

"I reckon it is," his father answered. "I heared Ambrose bringing the cows up a while ago."

Mr. Rabun turned back to stripping the limbs from a felled tree. His ax rose and fell in swift regular strokes, and the branches dropped neatly away from the trunk. Chad grinned. He admired to see his father work. Things never seemed to get all of a tangle for his pappy the way they did for other folks.

At last Mr. Rabun stood up and wiped his forehead on his sleeve. He looked around at the white-topped stumps and the sprawled logs. "We done a good day's work, Chad," he said slowly. "You was a big help. Two more days and we'll have us enough new ground for a cornfield."

Chad didn't say anything, but he was pleased. He'd worked hard and tried to do everything the right way, the way his pappy had taught him to.

Mr. Rabun slipped his shot pouch and powder horn straps over his shoulder. He shouldered his ax and then picked up his rifle.

Chad too reached for his musket. He hoped his pappy hadn't noticed that he'd almost forgot his gun. He hadn't had it long, and he wasn't yet used to fetching it along every place he went. Nobody in the Cumberland settlements went out in the fields without having his gun handy. At least not more than once.

They took the short cut home, through the woods. It was almost dark among the trees, and Chad wished they'd gone around by the edge of the field instead. The leaves hung dull and dusty, for it was the middle of September, dry and hot. "Injun weather," thought Chad, and he peered into the shadows.

Suddenly Mr. Rabun stopped dead still. Chad

halted too, drawing in his breath quick and tightening his hand on his musket. His father stood with his head turned, listening, his rifle half-raised before him.

"I'll shoot the first one with my musket," Chad planned. "And Pappy can get one, and while he's reloading, I can use the ax. That'll take care of three or four of 'em. And if there's more than that, I reckon we'll have to run."

And then he heard what his father was hearing, the little clucking sounds, like water purling over stones, that a flock of turkeys makes calling to each other. It wasn't Injuns after all. Chad let out his breath silently, and his eyes went here and there, trying to make out the birds.

Pretty soon he saw them, walking slowly, stretching their long skinny necks and small heads out of their big bodies to look around suspiciously, and then leaning over to peck at acorns on the ground.

Slowly, carefully, Mr. Rabun raised his rifle to his shoulder. Chad could see his father's finger tighten on the trigger and the flash in the pan when he fired. There was a great noise of gobbling and flapping wings as the flock scattered in every direction. But one turkey lay on the ground, and its wings beat wildly for a minute before it lay still.

Chad ran to pick up the dead bird. It was a gobbler, not a big one, but a young one, tender and delicious.

"Mammy'll like this," he cried as he lifted the turkey by its feet. "I heared her say just this morning she hankered for a turkey."

"Well, it was luck to find 'em," Mr. Rabun answered. "When we first come here, there was turkeys under every bush. Now here it is not but three years later, and a body don't hardly see one 'lessen he goes way off hunting for 'em."

He reloaded his rifle as he talked. "There's just one thing about shooting a turkey," he went on. "When you've shot it, don't forget to put another ball in your gun. I've knowed a heap of men got scalped because they got to looking at the game they'd killed and never gave a thought to reloading, and the Injuns heard the shot and sneaked up on 'em."

"You don't reckon there's Injuns around now, do you?" asked Chad.

His father looked at him soberly. "It's the Injuns you don't reckon are around that kill you, most generally," he answered. "But you remember what I say and reload every time you fire."

"Yes, sir," Chad answered solemnly. "I'll carry the turkey," he offered as they set out again. Mr. Rabun took both axes, and Chad slung the bird over his shoulder.

"You know what Amos Thompson said last summer?" Chad went on, keeping his eyes on the shadows ahead. "He said he'd seen a flock of turkeys kill a big old rattlesnake. Said they got around the rattler and took turns running and pecking at it till it was dead. Said the snake would strike at the turkeys, but it never fazed them. Do you reckon all that's really so, Pappy?"

Mr. Rabun pondered. "I've heard that tale," he answered. "I never saw any such thing, but I reckon it must be so. Amos Thompson ain't one to tell he'd seen something when he hadn't. There's some folks I wouldn't believe if'n I heared them tell a thing, for they'd be the kind of folks that might think they'd seen what they hadn't. But Amos ain't like that. If he says he seed it hisself, then he did."

Chad nodded. His pappy was always telling him not to believe everything he heard but to think things through and sift out the truth.

"You wouldn't reckon feathers would do much good when the rattler struck," Chad remarked, rubbing his cheek against the bird's soft feathers.

"You wouldn't, for a fact now," Mr. Rabun agreed. "I've seen a rattler's fangs go through stiff leather. But you study on it and you can see how it works out. Let a turkey ruffle up his feathers, and he's got a power of nothing and feathers between him and the snake. A snake's fangs ain't

hardly long enough to get through, no matter how hard he strikes."

They walked on in silence, leaving the woods and stepping out into the red glow of the setting sun. The tall grass at the edge of the field brushed Chad's buckskins with a soft whisper. A bobwhite called three times as they struck out through the cornfield. It was a big field, Chad thought

proudly, and there was another one this size near the creek.

Oh, his pappy was a fine farmer. In spite of the many Indian raids and having to rebuild their cabin and make new beds and tables, his father had managed to get the fields cleared and to raise a good crop. Not many in the Cumberland settlements could say as much, Chad reckoned.

They walked on between the rows of dry stalks. Chad's dog Tumbler came running to meet them, and in a few minutes they reached the cabin clearing. Ambrose was standing in the open door. "Here they come, Mammy," he called.

Chad got a whiff of the good smell of stew. He began to run, the turkey flopping on his shoulder. He hadn't known he was so hungry. And wouldn't Mammy be glad to see what he was bringing her?

Sarah met him at the door. She took the turkey and held it up. "Mammy!" she cried. "Look what Pappy shot!"

Chad frowned. She might at least have wondered if Chad hadn't shot it. After all, he'd fetched it in. The trouble with Sarah was she was *too* good at sifting out the truth, even if she was only nine. He couldn't ever fool her the way he could Mammy.

"Oh, Chad, ain't he a fine one?" exclaimed Mammy. "After supper I'll clean him and pluck him."

"Now go wash," ordered Sarah. "Milking's done with and supper's most nigh ready."

Chad yanked her pigtail. A body would think Sarah was a grown-up married lady, the way she acted. She was always bustling about, so busy and important.

After the bowls and spoons were washed, the Rabuns went outside. Chad cleaned the turkey and his mother plucked it, working quickly before the sunlight faded. Mr. Rabun stood in the clearing watching the sky for a change in the weather.

"I reckon he's keeping an eye out for Injuns, too," thought Chad, but he didn't say anything. His mammy didn't like to have them always worrying and fretting about Indians.

She had said, "It's bad enough to have the savages in mind all the time without dinging away at 'em every time you open your mouth. A body can keep a lookout for Injuns and still talk about something else."

When the others had gone in, Chad stayed a few minutes longer enjoying the cool evening air. An owl flew over his head with a soft whish. Stars were coming out, and the night was clear.

"Injun weather, for sure," thought Chad, and went in.

He swung the door shut and barred it with the heavy boards. He hated doing it. It was hot and close in the cabin with the door shut and no window and the fire going. But who would be fool enough to leave a cabin door open at night and the woods full of redskins?

Mammy reached up on the fireboard for the Bible. Every night she made Chad and Sarah read a chapter out of the Book of Kings or Chronicles, for Mr. Rabun wanted all his children to be able to read and cipher well. He himself had gone to school in Pennsylvania and learned Latin and history.

Folks in the Cumberland settlements often traveled a good way to have Henry Rabun read or write a letter. He could survey too and knew some law. Oh, Chad was proud of his pappy. He wanted to be like him, so he struggled with Jehoshaphat and Moab and Elijah the Tishbite. Folks had a mighty hard time in Bible days, it seemed to him.

"I don't reckon I'll let Chad read tonight after all," said Mammy suddenly, laying down the Bible. "I want him to card. I aim to get started spinning tomorrow. Sarah's got to have a new short gown. And I had it in mind to make Pappy a new shirt."

Ambrose frowned darkly. Every year he hoped to have some new clothes, but he'd never yet had them. He got Chad's clothes, cut down from Pappy's.

Chad grinned. He never had any new clothes either, but it never bothered him the way it did Ambrose. It was a funny thing for a five-year-old to worry over.

Mr. Rabun looked up from the ax handle he was carving. "I talked to John Hart the other day about buying a ram from him," he said. "He's leaving here and going back to Virginny. Then in the spring I can get a ewe, and we'll have wool a-plenty—if'n the Injuns don't get 'em," he added in a low voice.

Mammy sighed. They'd had four sheep when they came here in 1781, but the wolves got one and the Indians killed two, and the last one died right after it was sheared. So this wool was the last the Rabuns would have till they got more sheep, unless they used buffalo wool. Chad writhed at the thought. Folks said buffalo wool itched worse than cloth made from nettles.

Chad took the wool carders his mother handed him. He hated to card. But Sarah was knitting winter stockings, and Ambrose, who was stringing shucky beans on a long thong, wasn't handy enough.

He pulled his stool up on the hearth and laid the right-hand card close to the fire to warm. He took a handful of wool and drew it across the left card till it was caught in the teeth. When the right-hand card was hot, he began to stroke the wool with it, tumming it until the wool fibers were all straight.

Mr. Rabun held his wooden handle up and inspected it by the firelight. He turned suddenly to the others and smiled.

"There was a song my pappy used to sing, about a ram from Darby or some such place," he declared. "He was so big a heap of eagles built their nests in his wool or some such foolishment as that."

Mrs. Rabun laughed. "I remember that song," she cried. "His feet was so big they covered an acre. I can recollect the tune a little."

"Sing it, Mammy," begged Chad. He edged his stool back on the hearth. He was about to melt plumb away from the heat.

Mrs. Rabun hummed a little to herself, and then shook her head. "I can call the tune to mind, but I disremember the words. They were so foolish, they wouldn't stick in anybody's head."

"I reckon it would be fine to have a sheep like that," said Sarah. "We could all have new clothes then, even Ambrose."

Ambrose yawned. "I don't reckon we could card that much wool," he spoke up sleepily.

"And it would eat a heap," went on Mr. Rabun. "Clean up a whole savanna of grass in a day, I reckon. Then you'd have to kill it, else all the pasture between here and Kentuck would be used up in a week."

"Think of the mutton pie a ram like that could make," cried Chad. "Wheee, a whole cabin full!

Mammy could cook one as big as a flatboat, and we could float it down to New Orleans and sell it for a heap of hard money."

"I can't abide mutton pie," said Sarah, wrinkling her nose. "I'm sick to death of deer meat, but I'd a heap rather eat it than greasy mutton."

"And I don't aim to cook one that big either," laughed Mrs. Rabun. "Ain't no need to talk of eating mutton when we ain't got any. Well, that turkey'll make a nice change from deer," she added. "You was lucky to get it so close to the cabin."

"Change! Why, we had squirrels only last week," Chad pointed out. He had shot the squirrels his very own self.

"Oh, and they was good," Mrs. Rabun cried. "You and Pappy always keep us in meat, and we get more change than most folks. But it's been a long spell since we had turkey."

Ambrose yawned again. He had long since ceased to work. His hands lay still in his lap, and the long string of beans dangled to the floor.

Mrs. Rabun took the beans from him. "Go to bed, Brose," she said gently. "You can finish them tomorrow night."

Ambrose stumbled to his feet and climbed the ladder to the loft. They could hear him moving around for a few minutes, taking off his moccasins and breeches, feeling around in the dark for his quilt, and then he was quiet.

Mr. Rabun ran his hand along the handle to check its smoothness. "Casper Mansker says he aims to build a mill over on his creek," he told them. "Me and Brose won't have to ride clean over to Frederick Stump's for a turn of meal, if'n he does that."

"Remember when we first come here, how we had to grind our corn with a mortar?" Mrs. Rabun asked. "We was lucky to have meal at all, I reckon. But mortar-ground meal ain't nowhere's near as good as stone-ground."

She laid a piece of leather on the floor by Chad. "Put your foot on that, so I can measure," she told him. Then she cut off a portion and sat back down.

Suddenly she dropped the buckskin and half-rose from the stool. "Listen, somebody's outside," she gasped.

Sarah looked up in fear. Mr. Rabun moved quickly toward his rifle.

"Naw," answered Chad. "It's just Tumbler scratching. He hits the wall with his legs."

Mrs. Rabun settled back to her work with a relieved sigh. "I declare I wish I wasn't so nervous about noises," she remarked. She picked up the awl by its horn handle and began to punch holes in the cut leather.

Mr. Rabun checked the powder in his rifle pan, and he too sat back down.

A stillness settled over the cabin. Chad could hear the fire crackle and hiss and the soft sound of the awl in the leather. Sarah put down her knitting and climbed to the loft. Chad watched her with eyes misted with sleep. He reckoned he wasn't going to keep awake much longer. But he kept on working the steel teeth of the card again and again through the wool.

At last Mrs. Rabun folded the deerskin shoes and laid them on a shelf. "Well, you most nigh finished all the wool, Chad," she told him, looking with pleasure at the long slender rolls he had carded. "I'll start spinning in the morning."

She took the two cards and placed them beside the half-finished moccasins. "Ain't it been nice this evening?" she went on. "We ain't talked one single time about Injuns or raids or scalping."

"Maybe not," answered Mr. Rabun gravely. "But I hope you ain't forgot about 'em. They've not bothered us folks north of the Cumberland River very much this summer." He stood the ax helve in the corner. "They're due to give us serious trouble soon, though. And we got to keep our eyes and ears open."

Chad, stooping to put another log on the fire, reckoned that was all Cumberland folks had done since they arrived here, keep their eyes and ears open for Chickamauga Indians. The raids had got so bad a couple of years ago that many of the settlers had been ready to pack up and leave. James Robertson, the leader of the settlement, had talked them out of it, and most had stayed on.

But still the Indians hung around the settlements, and it wasn't a week passed but what somebody was killed and scalped going to the spring or working in the fields. That was bad enough, but the early fall was the time of year the settlers dreaded most. Each year since the white men had come, the savages had made a big attack in September or October. Everybody had

19

gone to the forts; their cabins and cornfields had been burned and their animals killed.

Again this fall a heavy feeling of fear lay over the settlements. Chad could see how his mammy fretted. But he couldn't help thinking things would be better now that he had a gun of his own, a musket he could shoot pretty well. Now he could help his pappy fight the Chickamaugas.

He kicked the logs in place, and Mrs. Rabun banked the fire with ashes. When she stood up, the room was almost dark.

"Maybe there won't be no raids," she said hopefully. "Maybe this fall the Injuns will leave us alone."

Nobody in the shadowy room answered. But when Chad woke later in the night, his mammy's words were the first thing that popped into his head when he heard Tumbler barking outside and the sound of a galloping horse.

Chapter Two

Chad was already feeling in the dark for his clothes when he heard his father open the door to the cabin. Then a man's voice came up to him, loud and excited. He couldn't make out what was being said, but he knew. Injuns!

Tumbler barked twice as the sound of hoofs began again and faded away. The rider was gone on into the night to warn other settlers. Chad fumbled into his breeches. His pappy would have a heap of things for him to do. He'd have to make haste.

"Chad! Git up!" Mr. Rabun cried from the foot of the ladder. "Git the others up! We got to go to the fort!"

"Are they close, Pappy?" Chad called back. If there was time, they could drive the cows to the fort with them. "Be they right close?"

But Mr. Rabun was gone. Ambrose still lay

curled up warm and sleeping. Chad shook him. He heard the shucks rustling in Sarah's mattress and knew she was dressing. In his hurry he got hold of one of his brother's moccasins and kept trying to shove his foot into it. He flung it down and felt around for his own. He put them on and tied the thongs firmly around his ankles. They were worn out but he'd need them, all the scurrying around he'd have to do.

"Help Brose get dressed," he told Sarah. "He ain't good awake yet."

Chad reckoned he wasn't good awake himself. His feet and hands climbed quickly down the ladder, but his head felt like it was still asleep in the loft and having a bad dream. Maybe he was just scared.

Down in the cabin his mammy was moving steadily about the room, gathering up the things she would take to the fort.

"Pappy's gone for the horses," she told Chad. "Quick now, drive the cows out in the woods. And don't forget your musket!"

His musket, where was his musket? He looked around in confusion, and it seemed forever before he spied it by the hearth. Grabbing it up, he ran outside. The dark closed around him, and he paused. The air was crisp, with a real smell of fall in it. It was as still as the grave, Chad thought with a little shiver.

He edged away from the cabin, his feet sliding on the chips around the chopping block. He gripped his musket tight with both hands and headed down the path toward the cowshed. A black shadow loomed tall before him, and he skittered sideways off the path, bringing his musket around. And then it came over him it was just the big elder bush that hung over the path here. He swallowed and hurried on by.

He wished he knew whether the Indians were close. They must be right close though, for his pappy didn't aim to take the cows. He glanced over his shoulder, and the dark seemed thicker than ever, thick enough to hide a whole tribe of painted savages and he'd not be the wiser.

It was at that moment Chad heard feet on the path behind him, running softly toward him, running quietly as only an Indian could. He leaped forward in fear, wanting to circle back to the cabin, yet heading straight toward the shed. Folks caught smack in the open like this didn't have a chance. He tried to scream for help, to give the alarm to his folks, but he couldn't.

The running steps were right behind him, and he could almost feel a tomahawk raised over his head, when he thought of his musket. He stopped, swinging around and bringing his gun to his shoulder, all in one swift movement. His finger was crooked on the trigger when something struck him in the side and Tumbler licked his hand.

"Tumbler!" Chad gasped. "You fool dog, you most nigh got yourself shot."

The dog yipped around Chad, and the boy bent over and patted his head. "I'm the fool, I reckon," he told the hound. "I might of knowed you wouldn't let Injuns come around without letting on about it."

He hurried on to the cowshed and took down the bar. Belle and Lutie stood side by side, breathing softly and chewing. He pushed and shoved till he got them headed out, but in the doorway Belle stopped and turned her head.

"Git on, Belle," Chad pleaded, slapping her bony flank. "I know it's queer, but I ain't got time to explain it to you."

The cows moved off through the dark toward the creek, and he ran back to the cabin. The horses stood in front of the door, and Mr. and Mrs. Rabun hurried in and out, packing the bag of meal, the long-handled skillet, the ax heads, the knives, and the quilts on the animals.

"Get that bar of lead and gourd of powder out of the loft, Chad," Mr. Rabun said. "Hurry! Here, Sarah, put them pots inside each other. And get Brose out from under the mare."

Chad fetched the things from the loft in a hurry. As he handed them to his father, he asked, "How close are they, Pappy? And who come with the warning?"

"William Bennett," Mr. Rabun replied, knotting a thong around a bundle. "He saw 'em crossing the Cumberland River, and he come to warn us. There ain't no telling where they are at now." He pointed. "Hand me that string of shucky beans."

He tied the dried beans onto the saddle. "They might be sneaking up on this cabin right this minute." He tested a rope. "Put Ambrose on Hector, and we'll git!"

"Wait! Wait!" cried Mrs. Rabun. She ran inside and came out with the wool they had carded the night before. "Law, I most nigh forgot it," she panted. "If'n I had, you'd all been naked as jay birds this winter."

"Did you throw some water on the fire?" asked Mr. Rabun.

"Yes, if the savages aim to burn the cabin, they got to make their own fire," she answered, and her voice shook a little.

Chad knew it was hard for her to go off and leave the cabin and all their things once again. If the Indians burned it, there would be a heap of hard work ahead for all of them. But he reckoned that more than this his mother was thinking of the first time they'd had to go to the fort. So many things had been burned, the little cherry chest from Pennsylvania, and the picture of his mother's mother painted on ivory, and the wedding cap with the lace and ribbons. The six pewter plates his mammy had been so proud of they'd managed to take with them to the fort. But the plates had been melted down to make bullets, and she'd never had another.

It was sad. Chad himself didn't think much of pewter plates and cherry chests, but his mammy set great store in such trifles, and he was sad for her sake.

Mr. Rabun helped his wife up on her horse. She took the reins, and the Rabuns started for the fort.

Chad looked once more at the cabin, a dark shape in the night. Well, if it got burned, it couldn't be helped. As long as there were trees, he and pappy could raise another one. He turned away and took his place at the end of the line. His pappy led the horse that Ambrose rode, with Mrs. Rabun following on the other. Sarah walked along with Chad, holding tightly to his hand.

At first they were all jumpy. Every noise made them start, even though they had Tumbler and the horses with them to give warning if the Indians were hiding along their route. It was so dark, and Sarah kept stumbling and pulling Chad off the path. But after an hour the sky in the east began to lighten, and things didn't seem quite so queersome and scary.

Chad could see Ambrose's fat legs sticking out from among the bags and pots. It was still a heap further to the fort, but he'd rather walk all the way than jog along with all that gear tied around him. He didn't reckon it bothered Brose. Pappy said Ambrose was so lazy he'd rather ride a cocklebur than stretch his legs walking.

It was broad daylight when they got to the fort. Tom Caldwell was looking out of one of the loopholes, and Chad threw a rock at him. Tom stuck out his tongue. The gate was open, and several men with rifles stood around among the stumps outside the stockade. They greeted the Rabuns as they made their way inside the walls, fashioned of ten foot high logs sharpened into points.

"Put our truck over yonder next to the wall," Mr. Rabun said, pointing.

Chad nodded. He was glad to be staying outside the blockhouse. Some of the families always tried to crowd inside, and it was so small none of them had space to turn around. It was bad enough being fenced in the stockade, like sheep in a fold, Chad thought, without being squeezed into the blockhouse.

"Get the meal bag down," said Sarah.

"Give me time," answered Chad. "And git out of my way."

"Rabun!" cried a man's voice. "We made sure the Injuns had you!"

Chad looked around. He saw his father step out to greet a group of men who had come out of the blockhouse. The man who had spoken wore a short sword at his side and had a pistol stuck in his belt. It was Abijah Boyd, who'd served in the militia in Virginia. He liked to have folks call him colonel, and he was always strutting around like he ran the Cumberland settlements single-handed.

Chad had heard tell Colonel Boyd was a fine, brave soldier, but he'd never believed it a minute. He didn't like Abijah Boyd and he never would.

"I hope you brung enough food and ammunition for a long siege," Mr. Boyd went on.

"I brung enough," said Mr. Rabun a little shortly. "Leastways I brung all I had. How close are the Injuns?"

"Put your truck anywhere you can find a place," directed Colonel Boyd, sweeping his arm around the fort. "We're mighty crowded. One new family since last fall and the fort not any bigger."

"Has there been any word about the Injuns?" repeated Mr. Rabun a little louder.

"Chad, git the meal bag down," pleaded Sarah, tugging at her brother's sleeve.

"Hush up a minute, can't you?" muttered Chad. He didn't aim to miss hearing what his pappy and Colonel Boyd had to say.

Colonel Boyd puffed out his cheeks. "Well, now, I ain't heard from Amos Thompson exactly where the savages be," he answered finally. "But I reckon I know a thing or two about Injuns myself. And I count on it they'll be here in the morning."

Nobody said anything, and the Colonel turned and surveyed the fort walls for a moment. "I reckon I ought to go right this minute and make out a guard list," he went on. "Tell you men when you're to stand watch."

"I reckon you better do that," Mr. Rabun agreed. Suddenly he looked over Colonel Boyd's shoulder toward the gate.

Colonel Boyd turned to see what Mr. Rabun saw. "Now what're they doing here?" he asked, adding gruffly, "They ain't welcome."

Chad craned his neck, wondering who in creation they could be.

The group came slowly through the gate. First a tad younger than Brose, then a woman holding a baby, and finally a boy not much older than Chad, carrying a crude bow and arrow. Dirty, white-faced, and spindly-looking, they stood just inside the gate, as if they couldn't take another step.

"Traitor ain't with 'em," the Colonel noticed.

Traitor Logan! Chad pricked up his ears. He'd heard that name. The Logans were woodsies who lived about four miles from the fort in an old cabin with the roof half-gone. Folks said the Logans were friendlier with the Indians than they were with white folks. Chad knew they'd never been here to Thompson's Fort before when the Indians raided the settlements, so maybe it was the gospel truth. His pappy said Traitor Logan had lived with the Indians once and that's how he had earned his nickname.

But Chad was disappointed that Traitor wasn't with his family. He'd like to see the man. Traitor must have horns and a tail the way folks talked about him.

31

Colonel Boyd stepped up to the gate. "Who told you to come here?" he demanded harshly.

"Amos Thompson," the woman answered faintly.

"Well, you can't come in," Colonel Boyd cried. "We're short of food, and you ain't brought none with you. Besides we don't aim to shelter folks in here that think more of Injuns than they do of their own kind."

"I reckon they're harmless," Mr. Rabun put in. "They've left Traitor to home. Or maybe he's left them."

The Colonel paid no attention. He pointed to the open gate and thundered, "You can just turn yourselves around and leave right now."

"Boyd, you got no right to say that," Mr. Rabun said. "You got no right whatsoever to run a lone white woman and three chaps out in the woods with Injuns around. It would be the same as murder."

"We don't aim to make no trouble," said Mrs. Logan sadly. "We'll leave. We'll leave right now."

Two or three other men had come up. From the way they looked, Chad reckoned they didn't waste any love on Traitor's folks. He didn't know what to think. It didn't seem right to turn folks out of the fort. But after all the Logans must be friendly enough with the Chickamaugas. They wouldn't be in any danger surely.

"There ain't no need for you to go," said Mr. Rabun. He stared steadily at Colonel Boyd.

The Colonel turned red and looked flustered. "I got as much right to put them out as anybody in this here fort," he said finally. "We can have a show of hands on it, if you're so minded."

"No, I ain't so minded," Mr. Rabun answered sharply. "I don't aim to be part and parcel of killing folks no matter how many of the rest of you be willing. I'll be responsible for these folks, and I'll see to it they get fed."

Colonel Boyd swelled up big and red as a turkey cock, but he didn't say anything. Mr. Rabun went up to his wife and spoke to her. Chad turned and began to unload the horses.

His mammy stood to one side. She had been listening to all the talk. "Open the meal bag and get Sarah her dollie afore she has a running fit," she said absently.

"You reckon we got enough to feed all them folks?" asked Chad.

Mrs. Rabun frowned. "Of course we do," she replied quickly. "I don't reckon it'll hurt us to go a little short for them. Your pappy done right."

And then she sighed. "Leastways, I hope he done right," she added, half to herself. "A fort's crowded enough with so many people and horses in a space this size. But when hate comes in the gate, half the world ain't big enough."

Chad took the meal bag off the mare and set it down. He untied the thong that held its mouth. Sarah plunged her hand into the meal and drew out a carved wooden doll. She shook it gently till all the meal spilled off the leather dress and then smiled at Chad. "She's all right, I reckon," she remarked.

"What'd you put her in there for?" asked Chad.

"Well, I didn't want to carry her," she explained. "I'm too old to play with dollies."

Chad laughed and pulled her pigtail. "Well, don't let her wander too far from the fort," he told his sister.

35

Later Colonel Boyd came out in the center of the stockade and announced that all the young 'uns would have to go for water. The small spring inside the stockade was very nearly dry.

"Git all the piggins and kettles you got and fill 'em up," he shouted. "And tie up your dogs; they're getting underfoot."

Tumbler complained bitterly, but Chad tied him anyway. Then he picked up the small kettle and handed Sarah the piggin. There were two big wooden noggins with handles, and he gave these to Ambrose.

Brose set one of the noggins down. "It's powerful hard for me to tote two noggins full of water," he told his brother.

Chad picked up the mug and thrust it back in Brose's hand. "You carry two," he said firmly. "When there's Injun trouble, folks have to do things that are powerful hard for 'em."

They set out in a long file through the gate. The oldest Logan boy stood watching. "I don't reckon he's got anything to fetch water in," thought Chad. "Next trip I'll get him Mammy's skillet and he can fetch his folks some in it."

Four men went with them, their rifles ready.

Chad was surprised. He hadn't thought Colonel Boyd expected the Indians any time soon, the way he'd talked to Pappy.

Chad glanced down the hill. It wasn't very far to the spring, but there was a heap of ironweed down there for the savages to hide in. He was glad for the guard. Maybe all the men didn't believe Colonel Boyd knew as much about Indians as he claimed to.

Tom Caldwell dropped back beside Chad. "I got something to show you," he said. "Man, it's something you ain't never seed before, I reckon."

"What is it?" asked Chad, but Tom shook his head and wouldn't say.

Billy Renfro called out. "I see you got yourself a musket, Chad Rabun. How does it shoot?"

Chad nodded. "It shoots good enough to kill a redskin," he replied. "How you aim to carry three piggins of water?"

"One in each hand and one on my head," answered Billy solemnly. "Watch out, Ambrose, I see an Injun in the bushes, and he's a-looking straight at you."

Brose plodded on, swinging his noggins.

"I reckon these Injuns come looking for Ambrose special," said Tom. "He's so fat and juicy-looking. They'll take him back to the Chickamauga towns and roast him real good and brown, and he'll meat 'em for a month or so."

Ambrose didn't say anything. One of his noggins swung out and caught Tom sharply on the shin. "Yeooow!" Tom cried, dropping his bucket. He grabbed his leg and danced around on one foot, shouting, "You little varmint, I'll whop you good."

"I never went to hit you," said Brose, looking innocent.

Chad chuckled. "Serves you right for joshing him," he told Tom.

Tom limped along with agonized cries till one of the guards told him to shut up and get on with the others. Tom caught up with Chad and said, "Me and you'll get in a power of wrassling this forting-up time. I figure I can beat you easy this fall."

"I don't figure you can, but I'll give you plenty of chances," Chad replied. One thing about chopping, it gave you wrestling muscles.

It was marshy around the spring, and Chad

sloshed through the cool mud to where the clear water bubbled up. The others crowded around to fill their vessels.

"I ain't used to doing this," grumbled Abel Adair. "This here is girl's work at my house."

Chad dipped his pot into the water, glad he wasn't Abel who had six sisters. One was aplenty.

"Don't stand in the water; you're muddying it," cried Mary Renfro, pushing at one of the boys.

Chad moved away from the spring, waiting for the others. A red-winged blackbird sailed overhead and into a clump of cattails nearby.

"Now, look!" shouted Billy Renfro. He raised a piggin to his head and stooped slowly, his hands feeling for the other two brimming buckets.

"Steady, steady," Abel cautioned him.

Chad set his water down to watch, pushing his bare toes in and out of the mud.

"Look out!" Mary screamed. The piggin wobbled unsteadily, and Billy jumped back from under it, letting it splash all over Abel.

"You did that a-purpose, Billy Renfro," Abel spluttered. He grabbed up a handful of mud to throw. "I'll get you."

"Watch out," said Chad. "Here comes Gil McKaye to get you both."

One of the guards caught Billy by the shoulder. "Stop that foolishment," he said. "This ain't no play party."

Billy nodded. Abel squeezed the water out of his linsey shirt.

Chad swung his kettle up into his arms. Something clanged dully against it, and Chad staggered from the impact. He looked down in surprise.

"Injuns! Run!" yelled Tom.

Chapter Three

With a yell Chad flung down his kettle and ran. That was as close as he'd ever come to getting shot, and he didn't aim to give anybody a second chance at him. There was a heap of hollering, and spring water and buckets went flying everywhere.

Somebody's piggin full of water caught him on the knee. He stumbled, trying desperately to stay on his feet, but the earth was slick with spilled water. A boy thumped into him from the side, and Chad slipped, sprawling on the ground.

"Git up, boy!" shouted one of the guards. "Git up and run!"

"What do you reckon I'm trying to do?" muttered Chad. He raised himself to his hands and knees. A bullet whined over his head, and he turned cold all over. He cowered against the ground, feeling as if every Indian rifle in the nation was pointed smack at him.

Once more he scrambled to his knees. And right there under his hand was one of Ambrose's tankards. Brose! Sarah!

What was into him, tearing off and forgetting the least ones? He looked hastily up the slope. There was Sarah, running up the rise with the other girls, hugging her piggin to her chest.

But Ambrose! Where was fat, slow-moving Brose? The Injuns would get him for sure.

Chad sprang up, but he couldn't see his brother anywhere. Could Brose have hidden in the bushes? He turned back toward the spring.

"Ambrose!" he shouted hoarsely.

"You dang fool young 'un," yelled the guard. "Do you aim to get scalped?" He gave Chad a shove that sent him stumbling up the hill. "Run!" he screamed in the boy's ear.

Chad ran then, taking off toward the fort like a canebrake afire. He had almost caught up with Sarah when he saw Brose going through the gates. Fat Ambrose had been the first to reach the fort! If he'd had enough breath, Chad would have laughed.

The men were closing the gates as he sprinted inside the walls. They held it open a foot or two

43

so the guards could slip in. Then it slammed shut.

"Bar the gate," ordered Colonel Boyd. "Everybody that's got a gun, get to a loophole. If them savages are spoiling for a fight, I reckon we won't disappoint 'em."

Sarah, still clutching her wooden bucket, came up beside Chad. Her eyes were big as millstones. But Ambrose was sitting by his mother, looking as plump and placid as a toad frog in a hole. Chad began to laugh.

"What's the matter with you?" Tom Caldwell asked. "It wasn't so all-fired funny. One of them bullets whipped past my ear and hit that pot of yours. And if'n you hadn't been a-holding onto that kettle, you'd be laying down there right this very minute, dead as a roof shingle."

"I know it," answered Chad. "It's Ambrose," he went on, grinning. "I kept a-looking for Ambrose, for I knowed in reason he couldn't run near fast enough to get away from them Injuns. And all the time, Brose was leading the way to the fort."

"He was running, for a fact," Tom agreed. "He was ahead of me, and I figured I was outrunning ary bullet them Injuns might want to shoot a second time. I reckon all that talk about the Chickamaugas eating him gave Brose a head start over us."

"I ran too," said Sarah. "I was skeered. But I saved the piggin," she added proudly.

"You done fine. I don't reckon nary one of us felt real brave," Chad told her. "Anyway I like it a heap better behind these here logs."

He looked around at the men taking their places at loopholes along the walls. Mr. Rabun went by and stopped to ask, "You young 'uns all right?"

Chad nodded. "Pappy, you reckon the Injuns'll attack now?"

"Likely not," Mr. Rabun answered. "I don't figure there was more than two redskins down there at the spring. Scouts, likely, getting the lay of the land."

"Pa says hit was some buck warrior looking for an easy scalp," Tom remarked.

"It might be so. And then again there might be a heap of 'em," Mr. Rabun went on. "A body never knows what Injuns'll do." He took Sarah by the arm. "Sarah, you go help your ma."

"Where you going, Pappy?" asked Chad.

"Upstairs in the blockhouse," his father answered, moving off.

"Can't I go with you, Pappy?" Chad called. He'd never in his life been upstairs. A body could see an Injun a mile away from up there, he'd wager.

Mr. Rabun shook his head. "There's too many up there now," he said.

"Come on, Chad," Tom begged. "Come on over here by the fence. I got something to show you that'll make your eyeballs stick right out of your head."

"Let me get my musket first," Chad told him.

"Aw, you don't need no gun," Tom answered. "You heard your pa say wasn't going to be no fight now."

"Maybe not," Chad said. "But I never had no gun last time to fight with. And if there's any shooting to be done today, I aim for me and my musket to be right in it."

He ran to fetch his gun. Sarah and his mother were away on the other side of the fort talking to Mrs. Adair. Ambrose and Tumbler were asleep among the quilts and bags. As he picked his gun up, he saw the Logans, sitting close to the Rabuns'

46

pile of goods. They sat like wood mice, so still and dull-colored a body could hardly see them among the rotting stumps.

The boy suddenly turned his head and stared at Chad. His eyes were dark in their hollow sockets. Chad looked away. He didn't know whether or not he ought to feel sorry for the renegade's son.

He trotted away. Tom had settled down by a hole in the wall where two logs didn't come together properly and left a gap. Chad peered out. There was nothing to see but the goldenrod blooming in bright lines along the edge of the clearing and a scarlet black-gum tree in the woods. Down the slope among the weeds lay the piggins and kettles and skillets dropped by those who'd gone to fetch water. Chad frowned. He wondered how long the fort would have to go without water.

"Lemme look," said Billy Renfro.

Chad stepped aside. "Nothing to see," he told Abel and Tom. "If there'd been an Injun, I'd of shot him."

"Yah!" jeered Abel. "You couldn't hit a tree was you standing right in the branches."

"Look here, Chad, looky here what I got," urged Tom. He held out his clenched fist.

"I reckon I can shoot the hind leg off a chair and it never know it was gone," Chad told Abel. "I can outshoot ary boy with six sisters any day in the week, any time of the day."

"You ain't never seed what I got, I'll lay," cried Tom, raising his voice.

"Why, my least sister can outshoot you," Abel began.

"I can see Chad's kettle, and it's got a hole plumb through it," remarked David Stonecipher, who had taken Billy's place at the peephole.

The others, except Tom, pushed up to see.

Tom stuck his fist in his shirt. "All right, I don't aim to show it to you nohow," he declared loudly. "I reckon you'll come begging for it when you get bit."

Chad grinned. "What is it?" he asked good-naturedly.

David and Abel turned to look. Tom held out his fist and slowly opened it. There on his palm lay a curious white stone, honeycombed with tiny holes.

"A rock!" grunted Abel. "You'd ought to be bored for the simples, Tom. It's naught but a rock."

"It ain't neither," answered Tom fiercely. "This here's a madstone I got from the stomach of a buck deer me and Pa killed over on Drake's Creek."

"A madstone!" exclaimed Billy wonderingly, moving away from the peephole. He touched it with a cautious finger. "I heared all my life about madstones, but I never seen one."

"Well, now you've seen one," said Tom proudly.

Chad picked up the stone and turned it over in his hand. It was a queer-looking rock, for a fact. But then it did queer things, sticking to a mad dog bite till the poison was all sucked out. He'd heard you could wash the stone off in milk, and the milk would turn green from the poison. He'd have to ask his pappy if it really worked. It seemed like it might, just looking at it, but then again there wasn't any reason why it should.

"I'll swap you a knife for it," offered David Stonecipher.

Tom looked indignant. "I've heard tell of folks

giving a cow just for the use of one," he said. "Ain't that so, Chad?"

"I've heared they was worth a heap of hard money," said Chad, trying to keep his balance. David was leaning on his shoulder, letting more and more of his weight rest on Chad. "But I ain't never knowed anybody that owned one before. Quit it, David!"

But David only leaned harder. In a minute he and Chad were rolling on the ground. Tom shouted something, holding up his madstone, but nobody answered. Pretty soon he put it away in his shirt and grabbed Billy by the leg. They wrestled together, all five of them, everybody for himself. At last they all lay around panting and weary and feeling peaceful.

"A body wouldn't think there was Injuns about," thought Chad, lying on his back and staring up at the sky, smooth as water in a bucket and blue as indigo.

But when a commotion started near the block-house, he jumped up, his heart pounding in his chest. It was the Indians! He grabbed his musket, ready to poke it through the hole in the fence.

But it wasn't Indians. It was Mrs. Adair. She

was crying and carrying on. Abel ran toward his mother, and the others followed a few steps.

"The cabin," she sobbed. "They're burning our cabin." Her husband led her back inside the blockhouse, and Abel and one of his sisters followed.

Chad looked off over the fort walls. A cloud of black smoke hung in the sky in the direction of the Adairs'. He was sorry for them, for the savages hadn't missed burning Adairs' cabin a single year. Once they'd done it twice in one summer. And this time Mr. Adair had built a big cabin with a lean-to and a shuttered window.

Well, they'd all been expecting it, but it hurt to see it happen, a home-place going up in smoke.

"We'd ought to go out and fetch in them kettles and piggins whilst the devils is busy burning up the countryside," one of the men suggested.

But Colonel Boyd wouldn't hear of it. "It might just be a trick," he said.

"But we got to have us some water soon," Mr. Caldwell declared.

One of the guards in the upstairs of the blockhouse called out, "Open up the gate. Yonder comes Amos Thompson."

"Open the gates quick," Colonel Boyd commanded, as though it couldn't be official unless he said so.

Chad pushed up with the rest to see Amos come in and to hear the news. Amos was a sight to see. Little and brown and knotted like a blue beech tree, he didn't look much like a scout and an Indian fighter. But he was, for a fact.

Now he slid in at the gate and stood looking around. He had on a breechclout and leggings, and Chad stared in envy. His mammy never would let him wear leggings. She said only heathens went around with their bare thighs and backsides showing. But wouldn't it be fine? And a short hunting shirt like Amos's, so torn it had to be held together with thorns, so dirty it might be any color on earth.

Amos's rifle slid through his hands till the butt struck the ground. He leaned on the barrel and glanced around the station. "You folks seen the smoke?" he asked. "You seen where the Injuns be?"

"Aye," answered Colonel Boyd. "How many is there?"

"Close to fifty, I'd say," Amos answered and spat.

"Fifty Injuns," thought Chad. It seemed like a heap. There were only nine men and about a dozen boys with guns in the fort. It was always like this, but the log fort made up for the difference in numbers.

"Did they go right on by Mansker's?" Mr. Rabun wanted to know.

Amos nodded. "Killed two men trying to catch some horses and hardly waited long enough to scalp 'em," he said. "They know this fort is the weakest. They'll be after us hot and heavy for a few days."

"How come the Injuns to know this fort's the weakest?" Mr. McKaye called.

Chad was startled. *How* did they know? Last spring there'd been a heap of men in the station when the Indians attacked—a bunch from Eaton's Fort had come by for Amos to go hunting with them. They'd stayed to help fight the redskins and then hurried back to their own fort.

Amos looked uneasy. "He knows the answer to that," Chad thought. "But he don't want to say it."

At last Amos said, "Somebody must of told 'em."

Chad felt a little prickle of horror run over his scalp. Traitor Logan! No wonder he hadn't come into the fort. He'd been out leading the Indians, telling them which blockhouse was the weakest, showing them the quickest, easiest path from cabin to cabin to kill and burn.

"I'd swear I seen a white man with 'em when they crossed the Cumberland," sang out William Bennett. "Is that right, Amos?"

"I'm a-feared your old one-horned cow's dead, Mrs. Caldwell," remarked Amos. "I seen her in the woods, stuck full of arrows."

"Was a white man leading 'em?" William Bennett asked again, raising his voice.

Chad slid his eyes around, looking for the Logans. Oh, what kind of varmint was it who could turn against his own kind and go around killing white folks like the meanest of the savages?

The hot midday sun beat down on them, and some kind of bug hollered and hollered. Chad held his breath. He could almost feel the others listening and waiting.

Amos scraped his foot in the dust uncomfortably. He couldn't lie for the life of him, and everybody knew it. Finally he said, "It's mighty hard to tell the difference between a red skin and a white when they're both painted up."

"It was Logan leading them Injuns and you know it," snapped Mr. Adair.

His wife gasped. "And burning my cabin," she added. Suddenly she pushed the others aside wildly and run up to Mrs. Logan. "I reckon you're happy your man burned my cabin!" she shouted. She began to weep, and Chad could see the cords in her neck stand out.

Mrs. Logan shrank back, and the boy stepped up beside her. His eyes blazed. Mrs. Adair raised her hand as though she were going to strike both the Logans down. The boy stiffened, waiting. But instead Mrs. Adair covered her face with her hands and sobbed aloud.

Chad felt sorry for her. But Adairs' wasn't the only cabin to be burned. Smoke rose from several places round about now, and it wasn't likely a cabin or a cornfield would escape. Traitor would know the whereabouts of everything.

Now Chad felt sure the Logans would have to

leave. Even his pappy wouldn't try to defend them any more. It'd be like siding with the Injuns themselves.

Colonel Boyd spoke out then. "We should never of let them varmints in this morning." He shouldered his way up to the Logans. "You can git and git quick," he said harshly. "You come with nothing, and you can leave the same way."

"We ain't done a thing!" cried the Logan boy.

"That's the truth," Mr. Rabun asserted in an even voice. "They ain't done nothing. I already said I'd feed 'em. You ain't got no reason to put 'em out."

Chad's mouth hung open in astonishment. He'd never thought his father would take the traitor's side.

"We'll see about that!" shouted Colonel Boyd. "Adair, how do you vote?"

"Turn 'em out!" growled Mr. Adair. "I reckon it was Traitor killed my brother last month."

"How about you, Renfro?" the Colonel asked.

"It'd be murder—a lone woman and three young 'uns without even a gun," pointed out Mr. Rabun.

"They don't mind murdering us," called out Mrs. Caldwell.

"Well . . . I . . . I . . ." stammered Mr. Renfro.

"You taking the traitor's part?" shouted Mr. Adair.

"No," Mr. Renfro answered quickly. "Turn 'em out."

Colonel Boyd smiled. "You going to be willing to go with 'em, Rabun?" he asked nastily. "You can take them back to their cabin, you're so worried about 'em."

A dull red flush spread over Mr. Rabun's neck and face. He looked twice as big as natural, and Colonel Boyd took a step back from him.

"Now look here," Mr. Rabun roared. He clenched his fists. "I may not be . . ."

But somebody interrupted. Amos Thompson walked up to Colonel Boyd and took his arm, and Chad could see the scout didn't favor gentleness.

"Ain't you forgetting something?" he asked quietly. "This here's my station. I own this blockhouse. I say the Logans can stay. Them that don't like it can leave theirselves."

"What's got into Amos and Pappy?" thought

Chad in bewilderment. "It's plain crazy to ask renegades inside a fort."

"Rabun aims to feed 'em," Amos went on. "And I'll vouch for 'em. I won't let them big fierce Logan boys git up in the night and open the gate."

He turned and walked toward the blockhouse, his breechclout flapping behind him. An angry buzz went through the crowd. Chad could tell they were madder than ever. But it was Amos's blockhouse, for a fact. And Amos was the best Injun fighter and scout anywhere around. The folks needed him. They wouldn't go against his word.

Chad looked around at the Logans, standing huddled together, skinny and white-faced. What in the nation had made his pappy take up for the traitors?

People began to move about. Mrs. Adair stalked over to Mrs. Rabun. "I never expected nothing else of Amos Thompson," she said sourly. "Amos ain't no better than an Injun himself. But I never reckoned to see the day Henry Rabun would act the fool. And he's a fool if he ain't worse!"

She walked off quickly. Abel was behind her. He gave Chad a long scornful look and followed his mother.

Chad felt something in his chest turn hard and cold. He wanted to run after Abel and tell him it was none of his doing, cry out that he hated the Logans too and would be glad to see them go.

But he didn't. He wouldn't let on he didn't think his pappy was right. He'd always been proud of his pappy up till now. And folks could cut off his arms and legs before he'd say he thought Amos and Pappy were wrong.

He turned his head so no one could see the tears in his eyes.

Chapter Four

"I don't want much," said Mr. Rabun. "Just some bread will do. I can't take time to eat proper, nor Chad neither. Amos says we better get to the spring quick, if we want water. We'll eat more later."

"Here's some ash cake." Mrs. Rabun held it out, adding, "Hit's cold, but it's fresh made last night."

Chad took his piece of the flat corn-meal cake. "I'm powerful dry, Mammy," he complained. "I don't know as I can swallow this here dry bread. Wasn't there no water left in that bucket Sarah brung up?"

"A mite," Mrs. Rabun admitted. "But I'll need that for mush for the baby," she said, nodding at the child Mrs. Logan held.

Chad frowned. It wasn't enough to have everybody hating him because of these traitors; he had to choke himself to death over them.

"I got a flask of buttermilk I brung with us," his mammy went on. "We'll use it now, for it won't keep much longer in this heat."

She brought out the gourd flask and handed it to Chad. "Don't take but a swallow," she told him. "A gourdful of buttermilk don't go far when you share it amongst this many." She gave him a look, and he knew what she meant. She aimed to share the milk with the Logans, and she didn't aim for him to say a word against it.

He peered into the flask. There was buttermilk aplenty for five—four really, for his mammy didn't care for it. He didn't dare swallow more than his due, though. His mammy would slap his ears off.

"It ain't I'm so mean," he told himself. "I'd share with any honest folks. But them!" He glared at the Logans.

The Logan boy got up and handed his ash bread to Mrs. Rabun. "Thank you, ma'am," he said stiffly. "I reckon I ain't hungry. Nor thirsty neither."

"Well, you'd better eat anyhow, Josiah," Mrs. Rabun advised him. "A mite of bread and a swallow of milk ain't much. But a body has to keep up their strength the best they can."

The other little Logan was mighty eager to keep up his strength, Chad noticed. He was gobbling his food down, stuffing it in his mouth like a 'coon eating pawpaws.

Chad swallowed his ash bread half-chewed, washing it down with the warm buttermilk that made him thirstier than ever. His mammy urged Josiah to eat, but he shook his head stubbornly. Amos Thompson came by just then and spoke to the Logans. He said something to Josiah that Chad couldn't hear, and at last the boy sat down and began to eat.

"Henry," said Amos. "Come along. I don't aim to wait no longer. You too, Chad. We'll want all the guns we got, if'n there's trouble."

Chad stood up, holding his musket. He shot a triumphant glance at the traitor's son. "I'll not have to share powder and lead with them anyhow," he thought.

He followed Amos and his father toward the gate. The other men and boys began to gather there. Amos was counting and considering. "Me and Rabun'll go for the water," he said, "along with Gil McKaye, Walter Stonecipher and his pa, and two or three of you older boys there." He pointed them out. "Boyd, you and Adair and Renfro and William Bennett get up in the block-house and give us some good covering fire."

Colonel Boyd didn't think much of taking orders from Amos, Chad could tell. The Colonel stood with his mouth open, trying to think of a good reason not to do what Amos said. But at last he followed the others toward the blockhouse.

Chad wished Amos would give him something important to do, even though he knew he was too young and his musket didn't have the range the rifles did. He reckoned Amos would let him stand here at the gate anyway. And maybe when their real attack came, he'd get his chance. He'd do something brave and famous.

He looked around the stockade. When they left the fort after last spring's Indian trouble, Chad told himself he'd come back sometime when Indians weren't around. He'd explore the block-house and visit with Amos. But he had never done it, never had the chance. He reckoned he wouldn't know the place all silent, empty, with only tree stumps and pokeberry bushes inside the walls.

Now it was so crowded it was hard to walk. People and dogs everywhere, quilts spread on the ground, and bundles piled on bundles. Six horses were tied in one corner and the Rabun's two on the side, with three more and a heifer due to calve in a half-rotten shed outside the fort. All the animals would have to have water before long. Chad hoped they could get it without any trouble this time.

He turned around restlessly and caught Billy Renfro's eye. Billy looked away quickly. Chad shrugged. "Billy Renfro's got no more sense than a hoe handle," he told himself. "Let him act that way. I don't care a snap."

It was different for Amos and his father. Oh, a body could tell Mr. Adair and the others carried a grudge. But they were all busy; they had fighting and guarding and important things to do. They *had* to work together, even with frowns on their faces.

But what was there left for a boy when the others turned against him and none of them would wrestle or run with him or borrow his knife or stand by him at the gate?

"You young 'uns there with guns, stay here at the gate with Mr. Caldwell," Amos told them. "Don't go outside and don't shoot us if'n we have to run for the fort."

David and Billy and Tom lined up in the gate. "They look mighty big, holding up them guns," Chad thought as he took his place to one side of them. "Won't none of us git to fire a shot even if there is any fighting."

Amos turned and called out, "Some of you folks let them dogs loose now. We don't want 'em inside the fort nohow. Them hounds ain't done a thing but eat. They can give us warning of the Injuns if they don't do nothing else."

Chad was surprised to see Josiah Logan get up and untie Tumbler. The traitor's son leaned over the dog and scratched the long soft ears for a minute. Chad whistled, and Tumbler leaped away from Josiah and galloped up to him. He grabbed the loose skin at the back of the animal's neck and shook him. "I'll take a hickory to you," he muttered savagely. "Quit hanging around that renegade."

The other dogs ran out the gate, howling and snapping happily at each other. Tumbler loped down the slope after them. Suddenly a couple of the dogs stopped, sniffing the air, then ran forward. They splashed through the spring and disappeared into the bushes baying. The others followed swiftly, though some of them stopped to lap up water.

"Quick!" Amos yelled. "Them red devils are close. We got to be quick!"

The men ran. Some of them stooped to pick up the scattered piggins as they ran. Amos hurried before them with his rifle ready to shoot.

The dogs were making a tremendous racket in the woods. Two of the men had already started up the hill with full piggins. Chad could see his father, closer to the woods than the rest, kick a bucket toward the spring for one of the men.

Suddenly over the baying rose the howl of a dog in pain. And right after that came a war whoop, a high wild sound that set Chad's teeth on edge. Two shots rang out close together. Mr. Caldwell began to shut the gate.

Now Amos was firing into the woods. He yelled something as he reloaded, and Mr. Rabun swung his gun around and shot. Chad moved out a step or two from the gate. He'd not seen a single savage yet.

The first two men carrying water jogged past him, and three more were halfway up the hill. Only Mr. Rabun, Walter Stonecipher, and Amos were still a good ways from the fort. Why didn't they run like the others?

Several warriors rushed from the woods, and a couple sprinted out from the weeds to the side. The Stonecipher boy fired, and one of the Indians fell, but the others came running on, so close there wasn't time to reload. Walter grabbed his rifle by the barrel and swung at the first brave. He missed and slipped to his knees.

Chad reckoned he was a goner. But Amos sprang forward and tomahawked the Chickamauga. He pulled Walter to his feet, and they ran up the slope. Mr. Rabun followed, turning once to fire. There were shots from the blockhouse, and Chad gripped his musket. He wished he was down there with his father, down there shooting one of the red savages.

Now the three white men were halfway up the hill with the Indians close behind. One brave

threw a tomahawk. Chad drew in his breath, it came so close to Amos. Another Indian stopped to take careful aim. There were shots from the blockhouse, and the red man dropped his gun and sprawled on the ground.

Still one big warrior ran on, almost within reach of Mr. Rabun. Chad moaned. Why didn't somebody shoot that big 'un? He raised his musket, but Amos and his father were between him and the Indian. He swung out to the side a few steps and raised his gun once more, hoping to get a clear shot.

Mr. Caldwell bellowed at him to get back in the fort. Chad turned. He hadn't realized how far he'd let himself get drawn outside. What a fool he'd been! Now he would have to run back without firing a shot.

And then he saw the Indians creeping unseen below the blockhouse and along the fort wall, coming closer and closer and getting ready to cut his pappy and the other two off from the gate!

Chapter Five

Chad was scared. He could feel his gizzard knot up in his stomach. But he didn't run. He stood his ground and brought his gun up to his shoulder.

"I can shoot that first one," he told himself. "I can shoot him sure as I can shoot a deer. He ain't no more'n a running deer." He swallowed and forced his knees to stop trembling.

The first brave coming toward him was painted with wavy red lines and a big white spot smack in the middle of his chest. Carefully Chad aimed at the white mark. He and the savage might have been alone in the world. He didn't see or hear another thing. There was nothing but that white spot and his musket's sight against it. Steadily Chad squeezed on the trigger.

The flint fell and there was a flash. Through the smoke from the barrel Chad saw the Indian slow down and a look of surprise come over his painted face. The brave raised his foot to take another step and reeled against the stockade wall, his tomahawk falling from his hand. He clawed at his bleeding chest. Then he slumped to the ground.

"I've shot me an Injun," Chad told himself and could hardly believe it.

The other warriors were coming right on, leaping over the one Chad had shot. Chad reached for his powder horn. He would reload quickly and shoot another. His hand groped at his side. His powder horn! He didn't have it! He'd left it lying on the ground, along with his shot pouch, when he ate the ash bread.

The Indians were almost on Chad before he turned to run. Amos and Mr. Rabun were hurrying toward him, and out of the corner of his eye he saw Amos slam into the first savage with his rifle, but he didn't wait any longer. He scooted past Mr. Caldwell and through the gate and stood there panting.

There was a heap of firing from the blockhouse. Everybody was watching the fight. They must all have seen Chad kill the Indian. He looked around expectantly, but nobody said anything. Nobody hollered "Good shooting!" or called him "Injun Killer!"—not even his mammy who was watching through a crack.

"You'd think Tom Caldwell would say some-

thing," Chad muttered. "I mind that time he killed a little young deer, and nobody took on over it more than me."

Somebody touched him on the arm. It was Josiah Logan. "Here's your horn and pouch," he said softly.

Chad turned red. He wished he could hit the traitor's son, drive his fist again and again into that pale face. He hated the other boy for knowing he'd been stupid enough to forget his things. "He ain't being good to me," Chad thought.

"He's just letting on how he knows I acted the fool."

He took the straps with a grunt and slung them over his shoulder. Amos and Mr. Rabun sprinted through the gate, and it was slammed and barred behind them. The men were panting; sweat glistened on their necks and faces. It had been a close thing.

"I helped," Chad told himself. "I don't reckon I'll git no thanks for it, but I helped."

Josiah spoke again. "I seen you shoot the Injun," he said. " 'Twas a good shot."

Chad glared at him. Wouldn't it be Josiah Logan to say something about the redskin and not decent folks? The praise only made Chad angrier. He turned and stalked away across the fort.

Sarah was busy getting the supper-meal ready. The turkey was cooking in a pot, and it smelled delicious.

Sarah said, "Brose, put a little wood on the fire. Hit don't seem like that fire's hot enough." She gave the turkey a poke with a sharpened stick.

Chad wished he had some water. He was hot

as fire, and his tongue felt thick in his mouth.

Mrs. Rabun came up and poked the turkey too, then turned to Chad. "I won't say nothing to Pappy about you forgetting your powder and lead," she told him. "He's got troubles enough without that. But a body would think your brain was loose in your head, doing such a thing! I'm 'shamed of you."

Chad bit his lip. Yesterday this time he had stood in the new ground, proud of his hard work and his father's trust. For a minute he could see the felled trees and smell the sharp scent of new-cut wood. He could hear the grasshoppers whirring in the weeds and feel the smooth ax handle in his hands. Was it only yesterday? It seemed like a year ago.

Now nobody cared that he was a hard worker or that he'd killed an Indian. Folks despised him. He knew in reason his mammy had seen him shoot the redskin. But she hadn't opened her mouth except to tell him he was a dunderhead, and he already knew that.

Brose came up and stood in front of him. "Let me load your musket," he begged.

Chad held the gun out silently. He reckoned

by this time everybody in the fort had heard he'd forgotten his horn and pouch and would be laughing fit to bust at him.

Brose stood there and poured powder down the barrel. "Is that right?" he asked. "Was that too much, Chad?"

Chad shook his head. He watched Brose fetch out a lead ball and a patch. "Don't ram it in too hard, Brose," he cautioned.

Brose nodded. Chad lowered his voice. "Did you know I shot an Injun?" he asked. "I did. I shot an Injun and saved Pappy's life and Amos's too likely."

Ambrose did not answer. He drew the ramrod out of the barrel and slipped it back in place in the thimbles of the stock. He raised the ribbed frizzle to make sure he'd placed powder in the pan. "Mr. Thompson's fixing to make me a powder horn," he said proudly. "He told me so."

Chad snatched the musket. "You ain't heared one word I said," he snarled.

Brose's round face never changed. "Here comes Pappy," he announced.

Mr. Rabun stepped in amongst them. He looked tired and worried.

"Where's the water," asked Mrs. Rabun. "I seen there was some brought in."

Mr. Rabun nodded as he sat down. "They aim to put it all together—what was fetched in and what's been dripping out of the spring inside here. Colonel Boyd will share it out, but there won't be much, not more than a gourd apiece, I don't reckon."

Mrs. Rabun looked up quickly. "A gourd apiece!" she cried. "Why, that won't . . ." She broke off, and Chad knew she didn't want the children to hear. She didn't want them to know that one gourdful of water was all they would have today and tonight and through the hot days of siege to come.

"Oh, it's all right," said Mr. Rabun wearily. "Walter Stonecipher's going to ride out for help after dark tonight."

Chad made up his mind if he ever got a chance to do Walter Stonecipher a good turn, he'd do it. "For this is the goodest turn a body ever did me," he thought. "Help'll be here before noon, and by this time tomorrow I'll be home and never have to see them Logans again. Or Tom Caldwell or Billy Renfro either."

77

Oh, but how could he wait that long? Quickly he stood up and began to walk around the fort. He couldn't stay still any longer; something in his innards kept squeezing up with impatience.

He walked over and looked out the hole he had found earlier when he and Tom and David and the rest were still good friends. There wasn't a sign of the Indian fight except a tomahawk lying by a stump. The Indians had taken away their dead and wounded the way they always did, to bury in some secret place, he reckoned.

It was growing dusk. The woods looked black and deep. There might be nothing more than 'coons and whippoorwills down there, the way it looked. But he knew better. Chickamaugas were there with their scalping knives and rifles, watching the fort. He was glad he wasn't the one to ride for help.

He moved so as to see along the wall outside where the dogs lay close to the walls. He could see Tumbler among the others, and he wished he could let his dog inside. The hound was most nigh the onliest friend he had in this world now.

He left the fence and crossed the fort to the spring. Here in the north corner the ground sloped away, and a ledge of rock thrust out of the earth. Most times the spring bubbled out through the rock and flowed out through the log pickets, but now it made a mighty little trickle. A piggin had been set to catch what water dripped slowly over the ledge.

Chad stared at the inch or so of water in the bucket. He was dry down to his moccasins, and the water looked powerful sweet and cool. But he wouldn't take it. Not even if he was sure nobody was looking, he wouldn't take it.

There were some deerskins lying in the mud. Chad knew what they were for—to beat out the flames in case the Indians set the fort afire. All of a sudden he wondered uneasily whether the savages knew they were so short of water. The whites had twice gone down to the spring outside the fort. Maybe the Chickamaugas knew, and tonight they might try to burn the station before help came. Maybe the Logans would give the signal when everybody was asleep.

His mammy called him to come eat, and he went back to sit by Ambrose. The turkey tasted as good as it smelled. He ate hurriedly, cleaning the bones and then waiting for his share of the

79

gravy from the pot. All the Logans ate hearty again, even Josiah. "That turkey would have made three meals for us," Chad thought. "And now it ain't nothing but bare bones. Them Logans is like locusts."

"If'n there was enough water, I'd stew these here bones for broth," Mrs. Rabun said. "But there ain't, so you might as well give 'em to Tumbler, Chad."

Chad gathered up the bones and went to the wall. It was so dark now he couldn't see a thing. He whistled, and only the sound of scraping claws and an eager whine let him know a dog was there. He couldn't be certain it was Tumbler, but he pushed the bones through the loophole anyway.

He strained to see something out in the shadowy dark, but it was black as the inside of a hat. He turned to go and found Josiah standing beside him. Chad scowled at him. The traitor's son was forever tiptoeing around. He ought to stay put and not go poking his nose in honest folks' doings.

Josiah held out a hand. "Here," he said.

"Here's a pebble. If'n you suck it, it keeps you from being so dry."

"How come you to know?" snapped Chad angrily.

Josiah shrugged. "I been thirsty afore this," he answered.

Chad pushed past him toward the fire. He could hear the tiny click of the pebble on the hard earth when Josiah dropped it. He almost wished he'd taken it, for he was dry as dust, for a fact.

Walter Stonecipher was getting ready to ride. His horse was saddled, and he was looking at its hoofs. It had been fed and watered a while back.

Billy and Tom, David and Abel stood around admiring the horse. Once Billy looked up at Chad and Josiah. He whispered something to David, and they laughed. It was a mean laugh. Chad knew the kind of things they were saying about him.

Without thinking, he spoke to Josiah. "Look at Tom Caldwell," he jeered. "He's patted that horse till it's a wonder he ain't give it the heaves."

"I reckon that's a pretty important horse if it's a-going to bring help," was all Josiah said.

Walter climbed up into the saddle, joking with the men and boys around him. Somebody handed him his rifle, and he took it and checked it.

Chad reckoned Walter had a good chance to get through the Indians in the dark. And once past the redskins it was only about thirteen miles to the Bluffs, the largest fort in the Cumberland settlements. But would James Robertson send help? Surely he would; there were so many men at the Bluffs he could spare some. Of course Mansker's Station was only five miles away, but they had too few to send help over.

The gate was opening now. In the dim light Walter seemed to sit mighty uncertain on his horse. "Maybe they'd do better to send Amos," Chad thought.

Walter grinned and waved around the fort. "I'll make it all right," he called quietly. Then swiftly he rode out into the night. The men shut the gate and stood listening. There was the sound of hoofbeats down the hill, a faint splash as the horse stepped through the spring, and then silence.

"He must of got through," thought Chad. "The Injuns didn't shoot at him. He must of got through!"

And now there was nothing to do but wait.

Chapter Six

It was dark in the fort. Only two small fires glowed and sent long shadows leaping along the wall. Chad could see Amos Thompson kneeling by one of the fires. He started to get up and go over there when two shapes appeared beside the scout. It was David and Abel; he could tell when they came between him and the fire.

He settled back down glumly. He had wanted to talk to Amos. The scout was always ready to tell a funny tale and help pass the time. And this was going to be a long night—hot and noisy. Folks moved about, and the horses stamped and whinnied. Lack of water made the animals restless. A baby wailed out, and a soft voice quieted it.

Suddenly David called plainly, "Tom, you and Billy come over here. Amos is a-making gunpowder."

Billy and Tom came on the run. Chad got half-way to his feet. He'd always wanted to see somebody make a batch of powder. Mr. Rabun always bought his mixed and ready for firing. Chad reckoned Amos was about the only man in the Cumberland settlements who went to the trouble of stirring up his own gunpowder.

Now the boys crowded around so they hid Amos. Chad stood up uncertainly. If he went over there, they might not notice he was behind them. It might even be, they would welcome him. "It ain't me they're mad at," he thought. "It's Pappy and Amos that took up for the Logans. And there them boys are, talking to Amos. If they ain't mad at Amos, maybe they ain't mad at me either."

But still he hung back. Chad reckoned it was hard for anybody to be mad at Amos long. And if he went over there, would Billy and Tom and the rest think he was trying to make up to them? Would they think he was doing the same as saying they were right and his pappy was wrong, that he was coming over to their side?

He shifted from one foot to the other.

"Chad, what ails you?" asked Mrs. Rabun

sharply. "You'd best get to bed. Get some sleep, if you can."

"It's too hot," answered Chad, and before she could say anything more, he stepped over to the fire. The others didn't even turn to see who it was, they were so busy talking to Amos.

"I always put in just the least little bit more niter than's in what you get at the trading store," Amos said. He picked up a sack, dipped a small horn cup into the bag, and poured the grayish stuff onto a deerskin sieve. "This here is niter, and it's got to be sifted," he went on, shaking the niter into a pot.

"What's in them other two sacks?" Billy asked.

"Charcoal and sulphur," Amos answered, going on with the sifting. "I make my own charcoal and then grind it up—make it fine as fine. I sift it in next." He measured it out, counting under his breath.

Dark specks appeared with the niter as the charcoal fell through the holes in the deerskin. "Now I finish up with sulphur and keep a-sifting it over and over till it's all mixed up good. That makes the powder even, and my gun don't hardly never misfire."

Was that all a body did to make powder, Chad wondered? Why, it looked exactly like what his pappy bought, black and fine-grained. It didn't look like much trouble the way Amos did it. Chad wished he could make his own powder. He'd have to remember to ask the scout where he got his niter.

"My pa says you got the best rifle in the settlements, Amos," Abel said. "Where'd you get it?"

Amos laughed. "This here old rifle-gun?" He touched it. "I traded it off a feller way back in Pennsylvania nigh on to ten year ago. He'd bought hisself a new rifle, and he couldn't shoot nothing with it. One day I was out a-hunting, and I killed me two fine bucks. He come up and said, 'Stranger, you give me them two deer, and I'll give you this here spanking new rifle, and nothing more said.' So I done it. It was all fancied up with silver doodads on the stock. I took them useless things off and dulled the stock with walnut stain, and it makes a fine gun. But it was no wonder he couldn't shoot nothing. Them silver things shined out like a light and scared off all the game."

"David Stonecipher!" somebody sang out, and

David groaned. "I got to go," he said. "My mammy's going to bed me down in the blockhouse."

Tom yawned. "I got to go, too," he said. "I been without all the sleep I can spare."

Chad grinned to himself. Tom was a sleepyhead, for a fact, and everybody knew it. He started to holler " 'possum!" at Tom, the way they all did when they found him sleeping, but then he remembered.

With the others gone, surely Abel and Billy would notice him, he thought. But they didn't. Abel was holding the sieve, slowly shaking the powder through the holes burned in the deerskin.

"That's it," Amos directed. "But shake it a mite harder."

The fire blazed up, and across from Chad the light caught something white. Josiah! Chad held his breath. Josiah crouched there listening, skulking around the boys just as Chad was doing. Chad frowned. He started to walk away. He didn't want to be caught acting like Traitor Logan's son. But Amos was talking again.

"I used to get my lead from a mine on Jack Sevier's land, over on the Nolichucky," he began. "But lately I don't. I knowed a chap once lived in a lead mine so he could have all the shot he needed. But I don't reckon it was so healthy."

He grinned. "He was a crazy old critter anyhow. Never would go down in the Great Bend country for game. Said he went once and them big mosquitoes like to of scared him to death. They'd lie in wait for game along the trails and leap out on whatever passed by. He tried tomahawking 'em, but they was too tough. And he tried trapping 'em with bear traps, but they kicked 'em to pieces fast as he set them. So finally he tried shooting them skeeters, but his rifle got scared and run off, and he ain't seen hide nor hair of it till this day."

Chad laughed. He couldn't help it. Billy turned and saw him. He drew his mouth down in disgust and moved further away from Chad. But Abel hadn't noticed.

"Didn't your rifle never misfire, Amos?" Abel asked. "If'n a body takes care about the powder and lead and all, will their rifle always fire fair?"

Amos chuckled, filling his horn with powder from the pot. "Oh, a rifle's got its own little ways. There's always something can go wrong. The more care you take, the less chance there is of it happening, but there ain't never been a rifle couldn't something go amiss with it."

He began to pour the rest of the powder into a leather wallet. "Now, if'n you want a piece that don't hardly never ever misfire, I can show you the kind to have. That there kind like Josiah's got."

He reached over and took Josiah's bow from him. Chad could hear Billy suck in his breath. Abel looked astonished.

"Ain't no powder needed, ain't no flint to pick sharp or get crooked, ain't no barrel to get rusty or bent," Amos told them.

"We got to go, Mr. Thompson," said Abel stiffly. "We can't stay no longer."

He and Billy scooted off into the dark. Amos shrugged and laid another piece of wood on his fire. "Whatever ails them two," he said firmly, "they'll get over it. A human being's like a rifle; there's a sight of things can make him misfire."

Chad didn't know what to say. But he knew in reason he couldn't leave now and have Amos think he was a bent-barreled rifle.

"Can you shoot a bow and dart, Chad?" asked Amos, giving the weapon back to Josiah.

"No," Chad answered. "I ain't never tried."

"Well, get 'Siah to show you a trick or two," Amos said. He got out a little pan and began to melt some lead. "He's as good as any boy ever I seen. Can make his own arrows, too," he added.

"I just reckon he can," Chad told himself. "As good as ary Injun."

"Josiah, you mind that time when you most nigh shot me out in the woods?"

Josiah grinned. "I made sure you was a deer, Amos," he explained. "And then it come over me no deer could be that dirty."

Amos laughed. "I kind of had it in mind you was a turkey," he went on. "You was moving so soft and secret." He turned and looked at Chad. "Josiah's been keeping his mammy and the others in meat for a longish spell now."

Chad was surprised. "Didn't your pappy meat you?" he couldn't stop himself from asking.

"Naw," answered Josiah bitterly. "He was always gone off somewhere. And when he was home, he didn't do nothing but lie around and sleep."

Chad stared. He wondered what it would be like to have a father who was a traitor and who wouldn't even try to feed his family. Wouldn't even try! Why, his own father would starve to death before he'd let his family go hungry.

Amos held his bullet mold while he carefully poured lead into it. "I'm aiming to buy Josiah a rifle," he told Chad. "He's pretty good with a rifle, too. But he don't want me to do it. He wants to earn it hisself. He's got some nice deerskins toward it."

Chad looked down at his own gun. Even with his musket, his musket that he'd never done a thing to earn, he wouldn't be able to shoot enough game to feed his family. No wonder the Logans looked so poorly, depending on Josiah and his bow.

"You must be looking for a fight tomorrow," said Josiah suddenly. "Making powder and molding all them bullets."

"Maybe so, maybe not," Amos replied. "But whatever happens, I like to be ready for it. Now tomorrow a flock of geese might go over. With all this here extra fine powder and lead you boys

helped me get together, I can shoot any goose a-going."

"And he kin, too," Josiah told Chad. "He kin shoot a goose flying so high it ain't but a speck."

"I seen him shoot," said Chad shortly.

Who was Josiah Logan to go around talking like he owned Amos and knew him better than other folks? But then he must know the scout pretty well, the way they talked to each other. And Amos must think right smart of Josiah. For a minute Chad was envious. All that praise for a traitor's son and not one word for Chad Rabun who'd shot an Indian and saved Amos's life.

"Why, I shoot geese flying so high, when they fall they get buried in the ground," stated Amos, rolling the lead ball out of the mold onto a clean deerskin. "You boys get ready to do a heap of digging tomorrow. I don't aim to lose my geese just on account of you fellers being too all-fired lazy to do a little digging."

Josiah laughed. "Tell us a tale, Amos," he begged.

Amos opened his eyes wide. "A tale?" he exclaimed. "I ain't no tale-teller. I'm just an honest hunter and Injun scout. Every word I say is the pure truth. I can tell you about journeys I've made over the countryside and game I've killed, but I ain't no fancy liar a-making up tales."

"Well, tell us about killing game," Josiah urged. He grinned across at Chad.

"I can tell about hunting bear," said the scout slowly. "I've killed a heap of bear."

He licked his finger and touched one of the bullets to see if it was cooling. "You boys think Injuns is something fierce to fight," Amos began. "But they ain't hardly a patch to an old he-bear that used to own Mansker's Lick and all the rest of this country around here. Oh, he was a biggety varmint. I reckon it was ten-twelve year ago I was walking through the woods here about one day. That bear jumped me, sprung out from behind a sycamore tree. Before I could shoot him, he snatched my rifle away and broke it across his big old knee."

Amos poured some more lead. "I turned to run, but that varmint grabbed all the trees and squeezed 'em so close together I couldn't slip through. Then he grabbed me and flung me down and most nigh split my head wide open. He ran up and down me like I was the finest kind of road. I bit his heel, but he kicked out two of my teeth."

Amos paused, shaking his head. "That was some fight," he said. "But I was getting the worse of it. 'Amos,' says I to myself, 'it looks like this is fare-thee-well.' That bear seen I was about beat, and he began to let out a war whoop, opened his big old mouth and hollered out. And every time he yelled, I dropped a handful of powder down his guzzle. Soon as he'd swallowed it all, I picked up a handful of flint rocks and throwed them down that bear's craw. Well, sir, them rocks knocked against each other and made a heap of sparks, and that set the powder off and blew that bear up."

He poked a piece of wood on the fire with his pan.

"And that ain't no tale?" asked Josiah.

"Well, now ain't I already said I was telling the truth?" Amos queried. "And let me tell you, it rained bear grease around Mansker's Lick for a month or so after I blew that 'un up. A real flood. I had to stay close inside a hollow tree, for I ain't a particular good swimmer. But when things quieted down and it was safe to go out, I went on with my hunting."

"Now I know I got you in a lie, Amos," cried Chad. "You know you couldn't go on hunting. You done said the bear busted your rifle."

"Oh, he did," Amos nodded. "I never used no gun to hunt with, I used my tomahawk."

"You killed deer flinging a tomahawk at 'em?" asked Chad.

"Well, sure now, I did," Amos countered. "Every time I come across a deer, I'd fling my tomahawk at him. Then I'd run and hold that deer in place till the hatchet got there. I killed a heap of deer that fall, but it like to of run me to death."

The boys laughed.

Amos held up his hand. "Not so loud," he cautioned. "Most nigh everybody's asleep. And I think you boys best get right to bed, too. We may get a fight tomorrow."

Chad and Josiah stood up. Chad found he was sleepy, for a fact. And hardly thirsty at all.

"And if there's a fight," Amos went on. "I reckon we'll need boys like Chad there, that knows how to shoot an Injun."

Chad didn't say a thing. That was all the praise and all the thanks he'd ever get from Amos, he knew. But what more could a body be than "a boy who knows how to shoot an Injun"? He near about busted with pride.

He and Josiah walked silently side by side. Maybe Josiah was a pretty good boy after all. Maybe he couldn't help it that his father was a traitor. "Anyway, it don't matter," Chad told himself as he fell asleep. "Help will come to-morrow, and we can get away from this here fort."

But what woke him the following morning was a commotion in the fort. He sat up on his quilt and looked sleepily around. In the dim light everybody was crowding around the loopholes, peering out through the cracks and crannies.

Chad leaped to his feet and ran to the fence. And what he saw made his horrified breath whistle out between his dry lips.

Chapter Seven

Down the slope from the fort lay a dark heap. Chad knew what it was at once. Even in the dim light he could tell it was Walter Stonecipher— dead, killed by the Indians before he'd had a chance to ride for help.

The sun pulled up out of the clouds and struck across the little hill. The light fell full on the body, propped up against a stump. Somebody moaned and Chad wondered if it was Walter's mother. Oh, a body might well cry out, to think how bravely Walter had ridden out last night, and now . . .

Brose pushed up against him. "What happened to his head, Chad?" he asked, squeezing his face into a crack. "What did the Injuns do with his head?"

Chad jerked his brother away from the fence. "Git away from there," he muttered. "There ain't nothing there for you to be gawking at. And stay away."

He took Brose by the shoulder and marched him over to the Rabuns' place. Chad sat down. His legs felt numb; his tongue was thick as a board.

Sarah was there, rocking the Logan baby back and forth in her arms. "I wisht we had a little extra water, so as I could wash this baby," she said. "This here's the prettiest little thing. If he was clean and fed good and had on a nice, clean gown, he'd be pretty as a red bird. Chad, look at them blue eyes."

But Chad hardly heard or saw anything. He was bewildered and scared. He wished he hadn't been so certain-sure that help would come. He'd counted too much on being gone from the fort by sundown, gone to be troubled no more by the Logans nor the other folks either.

"I'm thirsty," said Ambrose and began to cry.

"Don't cry," said Sarah quickly. "It ain't no use a-wasting water that way. Mammy said we could have most of what's left of the water this morning."

"Not now, we won't," thought Chad drearily.

"We won't get no help now, and goodness only knows how long that dab of water will have to last us."

Ambrose stopped crying and looked at his sister. "The Injuns cut off his head. I saw it," he said.

"Hush talking like that!" Sarah cried. "You'll give the baby the colic."

Chad gave a shiver. How in creation had the savages managed to catch the horse and rider? And however had they fetched the body up the hill without the hounds hearing? Was it Traitor himself who'd done it? Traitor would know the fort was depending on the rider to bring help. He would know they would think Walter had got through safely when no shot was heard from the Indians. Traitor must have planned it that way.

Chad couldn't blame folks for thinking hard thoughts about the Logans. It was hard for Adairs and Stoneciphers to see the Logans sitting here snug and safe in the fort, while their own kin lay dead from Indian rifles and knives.

Chad saw Amos go out the gate to bring Walter's body back. If the Indians were there, they didn't fire at him. Mr. Stonecipher was waiting with a blanket, and they wrapped Walter up and toted him over close to the south wall.

It was quiet in the fort. Everybody stood around, tense and waiting, and occasionally speaking in whispers. Two men had begun to dig the grave, and the sound of axes in the hard earth rang out loudly.

Josiah and Mrs. Logan came hurrying across the yard. "I reckon they didn't want to stand there and see Walter buried," thought Chad. "Well, I don't want to have nothing to do with them neither."

He got up and went back to the palisade to stare out through the loophole, his musket at his side. It was as quiet outside as it was in. There wasn't a sign of the Chickamaugas. It was plumb queer about the savages, how they could be all around, ready to fight, yet keep so quiet and patient in the weeds, waiting for the time they thought was best for attack.

He saw Tumbler get up out of the sun and go down to the spring to drink. The sight made Chad thirstier than ever. He didn't know how he was going to be able to go without water much longer. He wished he'd saved more of his water for this morning. But last night he'd been so sure help was coming, he'd drunk more of his share than he should have.

He could hear folks moving about now, and he reckoned the burying was over. Still there was no loud talking. Only Colonel Boyd seemed willing to break the quiet. "Amos, you and Rabun come in the blockhouse a minute," he called.

"The Colonel's got some big plan, I reckon," Chad told himself without turning around. "And we're sure going to need it, for I can't in reason see what's going to save us. If'n we don't die of thirst, the savages will burn the place down. Traitor ain't fixing to let them redskins leave here till every one of us is dead."

Thirsty or not, he reckoned he could still shoot his musket when the time came. He wished the redskins would attack and get it over with. He moved back and forth so he could see a good piece to each side through the loophole. There was something moving near the edge of the fort clearing, something stirring up the dry leaves. Chad poked his musket into the slit and aimed.

"Don't shoot," exclaimed Josiah right beside him. "It ain't but a ground robin."

Chad jerked the gun down. "I never went to shoot," he answered angrily. "I knowed right off what it was."

Josiah didn't seem to hear him. "A ground robin's a right pert, friendly bird," he went on. "Stays around all summer long and all winter, too. It's here when the weather gets cold and food's hard come by. It don't run off and leave hard times for the rest of us."

"Well, then it's a heap different from some I could name," jeered Chad.

Josiah's mouth set in a hard line. "I reckon you mean my pappy," he said. "Well, let me tell you something. My pappy don't ask my leave afore he does something, any more than your pappy asks yours."

"My pappy ain't no . . ." began Chad furiously and then broke off. It wasn't any use. There wasn't anything he could say to this woodsy who was probably half-Indian anyhow.

They stood, glaring at each other, and then Josiah said, "I didn't aim to make you mad. I'm sorry."

Chad was going to walk away, but just then he

saw Tom and Abel watching them, and something made him not want those other two to see him quarreling with Josiah.

"It's all right," he muttered and looked through the loophole again. In a way he was sorry he'd lashed out at Josiah. One thing a body could be sure about was that Josiah hadn't had any part in killing Walter Stonecipher.

"That's a nice musket," remarked Josiah after a minute. "Is it got a name? I've heard a heap of folks call their gun a name."

"Naw," answered Chad slowly. "It ain't got a name. I ain't done a heap of shooting with it."

"Amos calls his rifle Old Squencher," Josiah explained. "And Amos's friend, Abram Neeley, he named his Pretty Polly. She can girdle a white oak, take the scalp off an Injun, knock over a fierce catamount, bring down a flock of turkeys from the treetops, lay out a buffalo, blaze a section of land, and split enough boards to cover a cabin, all in one shot."

Chad grinned in spite of himself. "That there must be some rifle," he admitted. He looked down at his musket. "I reckon I could call mine

Ugly Tom or maybe a fancy name like Beelze-bub." Suddenly he held the gun out to Josiah. "You want to see it?" he asked.

Josiah took the musket and looked it over carefully. He stroked the barrel. "It's mighty fine," he said at last. "That there stock's walnut, ain't it?"

"Hey, you," somebody called. "Hey, you Logan boy!"

Startled, Josiah jerked around with the gun still in his hands.

Gil McKaye sprang forward and snatched the musket out of his grasp. "You seen him!" Gil shouted. "All you folks seen him try to shoot me!"

Several men ran toward Josiah and Chad. Mr. Adair grabbed Josiah by the shoulder and shook him hard. The others closed in around the two boys.

Chad was afraid. He wished his pappy would come out of the blockhouse. There was a look about all the men he'd never seen before, and it scared him plenty. And he wanted his gun. It was his very own. They couldn't keep it from him. "Gimme my musket," he said to Gil McKaye.

Mr. Adair pushed him aside. "You keep quiet, Chad," he said harshly. "You keep quiet and you won't get hurt. You don't need to get in this a-tall."

Chad grabbed for his musket, but somebody knocked his arm away.

Mr. Adair, still clutching Josiah, cried, "Git the woman. And somebody open the gate."

Chad looked helplessly around, his heart pounding in his throat. What were they going to do? Why didn't Amos and his pappy come?

Mr. Stonecipher was sliding back the bar that held the gate. Two men were hurrying Mrs. Logan toward the entrance. She didn't have the baby with her. Chad had a glimpse of his mother standing among the bundles, looking frightened but stubbornly clutching the baby in her arms. The other little Logan was nowhere in sight.

When Josiah saw his mother, he cried out and began to struggle, almost twisting loose. Mr. Adair put his hand over the boy's mouth and began to drag him toward the gate.

"They mean to put 'em outside," Chad thought frantically. "They mean to open the gate and push 'em out where the Injuns can get them."

It wasn't right. It wasn't right for all these men to shove a woman and a skinny little boy around like that because of Traitor. And all at once Chad forgot how scared he'd been, he was so mad. He ran at Mr. Adair and grabbed at his arm.

"You let him go!" Chad screamed. "He ain't done nothing!"

Mr. Adair pulled away, and Chad kicked him in the leg. The man turned and slapped Chad sharply across the face. "Shut up!" he snarled. "I done told you to stay out of this!"

Chad staggered backwards. He wished he had his gun. He'd shoot Abel Adair's father. He was plenty mad enough to do it, even if he couldn't see straight. But he opened his mouth and roared, "Pappy! Amos!" And even when Mr. Adair hit him again, he kept right on yelling.

Somebody grabbed him from behind. Chad kicked and struggled. Then a hand clamped over his opened mouth. He bit down on it with all his might. There was a grunt of pain, and Chad was flung to the ground. He sat up and was surprised to find he was crying.

Mr. Adair had almost reached the gate. Chad

scrambled to his feet, meaning to run to the block-house. He had to stop them. He just had to! Then he saw Amos coming out of the blockhouse, his rifle in his hand, with Mr. Rabun after him.

"Adair!" Amos shouted. "Let that boy go! What ails you?"

Mr. Adair stopped, but he still held on to Josiah. "We're going to do what's got to be done this time, Thompson," he yelled. "And we don't aim for you to stop us. Nor Rabun neither."

Chad saw Gil McKaye and Mr. Renfro start toward Amos, as though they were going to grab him and hold him, too. But the scout must have seen them coming for him. He swung around quickly and without a word raised his rifle.

"Don't shoot!" yelled Colonel Boyd.

Gil and Mr. Renfro stopped dead still. Chad felt the hair rise on his neck. Would Amos shoot down two men in cold blood?

The scout fired.

Chapter Eight

The noise of the shot was terrible in the morning stillness. It seemed to echo back and forth within the fort till Chad felt he was rocking dizzily around the stockade himself. The people stood still as trees under the bright blue fall sky.

Somebody shrieked, a long drawn wail that rose shrilly above the fading sound of the gunshot. Chad jerked around. No white man gave tongue like that. That was a war whoop!

He didn't know what he'd counted on seeing. He'd halfway made up his mind Amos had shot Gil McKaye. But the sight of all those painted brown faces crowding up over the wooden fence made him stagger like he'd been hit. Indians! The savages were coming inside the fort, and there was no stopping them! Oh, this was what came of folks squabbling and carrying on so hateful. The Indians had sneaked up and climbed over the stockade because nobody had kept watch.

III

One brave hung head downward from the fence with his foot caught between the logs, his arms swinging loosely. Amos must have hit what he was shooting at. And now there was another shot, and the savages all began to scream at once. Folks in the fort yelled too, and more shots rang out. But nothing stopped the redskins. They jumped down into the fort one after another, like turtles sliding off a log into the river.

Chad took a slow step backward, his eyes on the Chickamaugas. Indians in the fort was something he'd never even thought about, never even heard of before. He didn't know what to do when something happened that couldn't happen. Amos shouted out a command, but Chad couldn't make out the words, so he stayed where he was.

Now, above the other racket, he made out the frightened whinny of the horses. One broke loose and began to race around the station, wild-eyed and frothy-mouthed. It stumbled and dashed itself against the wall at one end and then turned to gallop furiously back.

"Hit's the Day of Judgment!" thought Chad. He was shaking all over.

Near him, Mr. Stonecipher slashed at a warrior with a big knife, and one Indian slammed William Bennett with the flat of his tomahawk. Amos battered at two of the enemy with his clubbed rifle, while one of the Adair girls tried to herd some little ones past and into the blockhouse.

It didn't seem real to Chad, none of it did. Since he'd waked this morning and seen Walter Stonecipher lying dead and had fought to keep the Logans from being put out the gate, it had all been one wild, foolish dream, a nightmare to forget.

But he knew he had to do something. He didn't know what, in all this noise and confusion. Then he saw an Indian coming straight at him. He stood there stupidly, staring and trying to collect his wits. His musket! Gil McKaye had gone off with his musket and left him to fight the savages with only a knife he hadn't sharpened in weeks!

It was a bandy-legged Indian coming toward him, broad as a cabin and carrying a tomahawk. Chad turned to run, but he was caught. The fence wasn't five feet behind him, and everywhere he looked there were more Indians. He yelled and turned toward the bowlegged brave once more.

The Indian raised his hatchet, ready to send it slicing into Chad's head. The boy threw up a hand to ward off the blow, cowering backward. He'd give anything to be able to shut his eyes, black out the sight of that sharp-edged blade waiting to end his life, but he couldn't. He just kept on looking as the Indian came nearer.

Chad didn't even hear the sound of hoofs till the maddened horse was right on them. Neither did the Indian. The beast ran the redskin down and one of the hoofs caught him squarely on the forehead.

Chad shuddered from head to foot and leaned weakly against the wall. He'd been lucky as a shilling piece, but it couldn't happen to him again. He'd have to get to the blockhouse. He couldn't just stand around without his musket.

Somebody grabbed him just then and scared him so he almost fell on the ground. It was Gil McKaye. "Yonder's your musket," he panted. "It's safe. Git it and git in the blockhouse."

He ran off, and Chad sprinted for his gun. He grabbed it up with a sob of relief. The feel of it in his hands gave him back his courage. He knew what to do now. He wouldn't run and hide

115

in the blockhouse. Let the women and young 'uns
do that. He was nearabout a man grown. He'd
killed one Indian and he could mighty well kill
another, easy as not.

He looked up to see Mrs. Renfro struggling
with a brave right in front of him. The Indian
had a knife in his hand, but Mrs. Renfro had a
chopping ax. As the brave rushed in and grabbed
her by the hair, she swung her ax around and
buried the blade in his shoulder.

"Mammy," thought Chad. "Mammy's so little
and timid, I misdoubt she could fight so brave
as Mrs. Renfro."

He ought to make sure that she and Sarah and
Ambrose were safe in the blockhouse, and the
Logans, too. He looked hurriedly around, but he
couldn't see a sign of them. They must have
already run inside.

But then right at the blockhouse he saw his
mammy, and he cried out in dismay. One of the
Indians darted up behind her as she pushed
Robert Logan inside. At that moment she turned,
and Chad saw she was holding a skillet. She
pounded it into the Indian's face and sent him

staggering backwards. The door opened wider, and she scooted through.

The Indian crouched, touching his painted face. Chad raised his rifle and shot the warrior. He began to reload, trying hard to keep his hands from trembling. He could fight as well as the next one, he knew, and there wasn't any call for him to be scared. His mammy was brave, and he was, too.

"Watch out behind you, Chad," he heard his father shout.

Chad swung around. A Chickamauga had climbed over the fence behind him and stood balanced there with a rifle aimed smack at him. Chad crammed a bullet into the end of the barrel before he realized he hadn't put any powder in first. It was useless to him now. He sprang aside and the red man twisted, following him with his gun.

A shot rang out, and the brave crumpled. He fell on the sharpened points of the pickets with a scream. Chad knew it was his father who had fired. He shook the bullet out of his musket and loaded properly. Maybe he wasn't so all-fired clever after all. He'd come mighty close to getting killed right then and mostly out of carelessness.

Somebody yelled something about the gate.

Chad looked around, and his heart almost came up into his mouth. Two of the savages were sliding the heavy crossbar from its place. A few more feet and the gate would be opened. Then nothing could keep the rest of the savages from rushing in and massacring all the whites.

There was a shot, and one of the Indians slumped against the gate, sliding down almost to the ground. Then he reached up and grabbed the bar. He pulled himself to his feet and went on struggling to get the gate open. Blood ran in a long stream down his back and across his breechclout.

The Indians outside began pushing against the gates, and they buckled inward. The bar slid the last foot, and the gate opened. Three savages crowded in, but two fell as they got inside. Colonel Boyd rushed up and cut at the third one with his short sword. Amos and another man stood in front of the gate and beat with their rifles at the Indians as they came in.

Mr. Caldwell shoved against the gate, trying desperately to close it. Mr. Rabun came to help, and in a moment they had the gate shut and the bar back in place.

One of the Indians had got past Amos. But now he sprang by Chad and leaped for the fence. He caught the top and pulled himself quickly up between the pointed logs.

Chad aimed carefully and was ready to fire when the brave hauled himself around and sent his tomahawk skimming by Chad's head. Chad couldn't get out of the way quick enough, tripping over his own feet. The savage leaped from the fence and was gone.

"Dang it!" Chad muttered. "There's one more to fight later on. I ought not to be so slow aiming."

It wasn't till it got quiet in the fort that Chad knew it was all over, that they had fought the Indians off and saved the station. His legs felt weak and trembly. He was sweating, and when he wiped his hand over his face, it came away smudged with black gunpowder. His lips were cracked and dry, and he longed for a drink of water. How long had it been since he'd had all the cold water he could hold?

He saw Josiah sitting crouched by the block-house, staring down at the ground. Chad went over and eased down beside him. Josiah didn't look up or speak.

A dead Indian lay sprawled not far away. Chad could see the paint cracked and peeling on his body. The scalp lock on the crown of the Chickamauga's head was small and round, and the black hair stood up stiffly.

The Indian didn't look fierce any more. He didn't look particularly cruel or strong either. He just looked dead, Chad thought, and moved his eyes away.

"That was some fight," he said to Josiah finally. "Where was you while it was going on?"

"I was here," Josiah answered after a minute.

Chad was astonished. "Right here? Setting right here while the fight was going on? You was lucky you wasn't killed."

Josiah lifted his head. "I don't reckon I was so lucky," he said. "I might be better off dead than staying here where folks all wish I was dead anyhow."

He glared fiercely around the fort. "I ain't

done one thing to these here folks. I ain't done nothing all my life but try to look after my mammy and the young 'uns. And all these here folks hate me so much they aimed to put me and my mammy out where the Injuns could get us."

Chad didn't say anything. He was wondering what it would be like to be Josiah and have folks hating you and trying to hurt you and your mother. It was more than he wanted to think about.

"I don't reckon everybody hates you," he said slowly. "I don't hate you. My folks don't hate you, not even Ambrose. And Amos don't hate you, and he's the best Injun scout in creation."

Josiah drew a long trembling breath. "That's right," he said and smiled a little bit. "We got some friends. And I reckon them other folks can't help being ornery. But I'm mighty proud you don't hate me. All you Rabuns is been good to us."

"We ain't done nothing," Chad answered gruffly. "We don't want no thanks." He was thinking back how he hadn't always been good to Josiah. He hoped the other boy didn't remember.

Two men came over to tote off the dead Indian.

The women and children began to leave the blockhouse. They looked around as though they didn't know what awful thing they might see.

Chad stood up when he saw his mother come out. "Come on," he said to Josiah. "Let's go get a drink afore I turn into a puddle of dust and get blown away. There's a swallow or so of water left, I reckon."

Sarah was already tidying up the Rabuns' possessions. Chad reckoned he'd have to help her soon as he got his water.

"Mr. Renfro got a real bad cut on his arm," she told them. "I reckon he won't do no more fighting this day. Ambrose, move. And Gil McKaye got a ball in his leg, and it serves him right, though I'm glad he ain't bad hurt. Ambrose, *move!*"

Ambrose stood right where he was. The tears poured steadily down his cheeks.

"Brose, whatever's the matter?" asked Mrs. Rabun.

"I'm thirsty," sobbed Ambrose.

"Me, too, but it don't help none to cry," Chad remarked.

"Well, I reckon you can all have the least little

sip of water," Mrs. Rabun said. "But Ambrose, you got to stop that crying first."

"He ain't stopped crying hardly since he got up," said Sarah.

"They can have my share of the water, Mrs. Rabun," Josiah spoke up. "I didn't hardly drink none last night. There's aplenty for them. I ain't thirsty none."

"We don't need to take your share," Mrs. Rabun began. "We can . . ."

She broke off, and Chad could hear her draw in her breath in dismay. He turned to look. There was the big water gourd lying on its side, cracked in two, and all the water spilled away onto the dry earth.

Chapter Nine

"It must of been that horse done it, the one that got loose," Mrs. Rabun said, lifting the broken gourd.

Chad stared at the wet patch of earth. What had happened to the Rabuns? They used not to have bad luck like this. Things used to go right for the Rabuns. Even when they'd had to fort up before and the Indians had burned their cabin, Chad had felt like it didn't matter, he and his pappy would set things right.

But now he was ready to give up. It was just more than a body could stand, having things go wrong all the time. Was it taking up with the Logans that had brought the Rabuns bad luck? He glanced over at Josiah. For a fact, nothing had been right since the moment they had laid eyes on these skinny woodsies.

Then he felt ashamed of himself, taking on like that. Josiah had never once complained, yet he was a heap worse off than Chad. And all the folks in the fort had had their share of bad luck, too. Chad deemed the Rabuns were having no harder time than the rest, and not near as bad as some. At least they were all still alive and kicking.

Ambrose began to bawl louder than ever. "Now quit that," said Mrs. Rabun sharply. She gave his shoulder a fierce shake. Chad was surprised. His mammy was hardly ever so short-tempered. She was just tired and thirsty like everybody else, he reckoned, and a heap more worried than she let on.

Ambrose gulped and held his breath. Mrs. Rabun looked down at him, and her face softened. "There wasn't hardly enough water in that gourd to fill a thimble," she told him soothingly. "And you ain't going to miss that little drop."

That was the truth, Chad reckoned. But still, when a body had his mouth all ready for a drink, it was worrisome to do without. He looked around for a pebble to suck, the way Josiah had told him to. He found one and put it in his mouth. He tried hard to suck it, but his tongue was so dry, he couldn't seem to get the pebble wet, so he spat it out.

Then he saw Mrs. Bennett coming toward them with a small gourd in her hands. She carried it so carefully, Chad knew she must have water in it.

"I brung the least ones some water," she said a little shyly. "I seen your gourd got broke. We're all nigh growed in our family and can do without better than the little ones."

"Well, you was mighty good," Mrs. Rabun told her. "The young 'uns been crying and crying for a drink. I don't know however to thank you."

"That's all right," replied Mrs. Bennett. She watched while Sarah and Ambrose and the two little Logans drank.

Chad turned his head away and tried hard to think about something else, anything at all but water. He wasn't one of the least ones, and he knew it.

When all the water was gone, Mrs. Bennett took back the gourd. She stood there a minute, looking uneasy, and finally she burst out. "I'm sorry for what us folks here in the fort has done. We was wrong. When I seen all them growed men pushing that little boy, I knowed right then we was wrong as could be."

She hurried off, and Chad watched her go. He must be like Mrs. Bennett, he thought. It was seeing Mr. Adair shoving Josiah along that had made him know things weren't right, that had made him fight Mr. Adair and holler for Amos and Mr. Rabun. Now he wondered how many more in the fort felt that way.

Oh, it was easy to think a boy was the same as his pa. Didn't he know that? Hadn't all the folks in the fort thought he was taking up for the Logans just because his pappy was? But it hadn't been true. And now he knew it was wrong to think a boy was good just because his pappy was good. And it was worse to think a boy was bad, was a savage and a traitor, because his father was.

The Logans hadn't done anything mean. They hadn't done anything but come to the station asking shelter. Whatever had made folks think Josiah was wicked?

There was a yell from outside, and somebody at one of the loopholes fired a rifle. The man swore and began quickly to reload. "I'll get that rascal this time," he said grimly.

Chad ran to see, and a lot of the men and older boys crowded up, too.

At the foot of the slope, down by the big spring, an Indian stood holding an iron pot. It looked like the one Chad had carried to the spring. The brave stooped and filled it with water.

"White man thirsty?" he yelled. "Much water here." Laughing, he tilted the pot and poured the water into the dust.

Chad stared at the cool stream. In all the world there was water aplenty, bubbling up out of springs and over stones, tumbling along in creeks, lying dark and silent in wells. And here he was, dry as sand, watching this Chickamauga spill water onto the dead grass and not able to get a drop. He swallowed, and his throat seemed to crack in a hundred places inside. His mouth burned and stung with thirst.

There was another shot from the fort, but the Indian never flinched. He knew he was safely out of rifle range there at the bottom of the hill. He filled the kettle again.

"Come get water," he called, and Chad could hear the water plainly as it splashed onto the ground.

Chad went away then, but the Indian stayed quite a spell, yelling and laughing. Amos told the men to quit wasting shot on him, but every once in a while one of them would get riled at the savage and blast away.

His mammy gave Chad some bread to eat, but he gave it back to her. "I'm too dry; I can't swallow it," he told her.

"Well, try to get some sleep then," she said. "You'd ought to save your strength somehow."

Sarah and the little Logans were asleep, and even Josiah sat hunched up with his eyes closed, though Chad doubted if he was sleeping. Chad stretched out by Brose, but he couldn't stay still, much less get to sleep. The sun was too almighty hot and bright; it burned through his closed lids and right into his brain. And he most nigh choked, trying to swallow lying down.

He could hear William Bennett's oldest boy and Mr. McKaye quarreling about somebody stepping on somebody's foot. Chad sat up and watched them. There were almost always squabbles before the families left the fort, everybody so jammed up together for so long. He was surprised there hadn't been more trouble. Thirst was making all of them feisty, like the horses, which were half-mad and had to be tied far away from each other to keep them from fighting.

Chad got up and wandered around. Folks who weren't asleep sat gazing straight ahead, their eyes dazed and their faces gaunt with weariness. They didn't even bother to brush away the flies that crawled over them. They hadn't picked up their bundles, scattered in the morning's fight. Chad hadn't ever seen folks in the fort act like this. But they'd never lacked water before, nor had the redskins come right inside the walls.

He hated seeing them look that way, these folks who'd always been so brave and lively. It gave him a cold feeling in his chest. Maybe when the Indians attacked again, not a soul would be able to rise up and fight.

He had to step over Tom Caldwell, asleep on the bare ground, and for a few minutes he considered stepping on him. That would make a little excitement and give him a chance to call Tom all the hateful things he'd thought up to call him.

But he didn't. Tom hadn't really acted any meaner than the rest of the folks here. And the Indians could give him excitement enough, he reckoned, did he crave such.

The dead bodies of the Indians had been stacked by the gate. Chad didn't see why they couldn't be flung outside now, instead of waiting till dark. He noticed that one of the redskins had been scalped. "Some folks ain't no better than savages theirselves," he thought and wondered who had done such a thing.

Then he spied Amos sitting on a stump cleaning his rifle. Chad went up to him.

"Watch out thar, boy!" cried Amos. "You like to of stepped on my old black hat. And it would of bit you good, if you had."

Chad grinned. "I figured it was so old, it had lost all its teeth," he remarked.

Amos picked up his hat and dusted it off. "Got every tooth it ever had," he exclaimed and put it on. "Where's Josiah?"

"Sleep, I reckon," Chad answered. "I didn't feel much like sleeping."

Amos nodded. "I'm most nigh too restless to stay in one place myself," he told Chad. "Come on, let's me and you go up in the blockhouse."

Chad followed Amos into the building. The floor was covered with quilts and young 'uns. Mrs. Stonecipher was lying on a pallet in the corner with her back to the room. Gil McKaye was propped up on the puncheon table. Colonel Boyd stood beside him with a knife in his hand, ready to cut the rifle ball out of Gil's wound.

The ladder to the second story was just inside the doorway. Amos went up it, his rifle bumping against the rungs, and Chad came right after him.

Mr. Adair was leaning against the wall and yawning. "I'm sure glad to see you, Amos," he said. "I most nigh been to sleep twice, just standing up here."

He didn't look at Chad. "I reckon he don't like to think about how he knocked me around this morning," Chad thought. "And I reckon I don't want to think about kicking him. Or how I aimed to shoot him."

It was terrifying to remember. Mr. Adair was a good man who had once walked three miles through the snow to bring Chad some remedies when he had a fever. What had happened to all the folks at the fort?

Mr. Adair disappeared down the ladder. Chad looked around and was a mite disappointed. It didn't look any different from any other room, except that all down each chinked log wall were loopholes, some high and others low. And here close to the outside walls there were wide cracks in the floor where the second story stuck out over the lower part of the blockhouse. Chad walked along the slits, seeing how easy it would be to shoot down on any savage skulking along the fort wall below.

"How long you reckon we can hold out here, without no water?" he asked Amos suddenly.

"Long enough, I reckon," Amos answered. "I aim to go for help soon as it's dark enough to slip away. And I figure you'll be home tomorrow without fail."

"Go for help," repeated Chad. "Do you reckon you'll make it?" He would hate for Amos to die the way Walter Stonecipher had.

"I'll make it, never you fear," Amos replied. "Me and Old Squencher been through a heap of hard times. We're tough." He patted his rifle.

"I wisht I had a rifle," Chad said. "A musket's all right, I reckon, but a body can't shoot near so far nor so good with one."

"That's right," Amos replied. "But you ain't rightly old enough for a rifle yet." He rumpled

Chad's hair and laughed. "Though I 'low a boy old enough to fight Injuns is old enough to own a rifle."

"Do you aim to get Josiah a rifle, for a fact?" asked Chad.

Amos gave him a queer look. "I don't know why not," he answered. "Josiah's a good boy. He needs him a gun bad as anybody I ever seen. He's got his mammy and them young 'uns to look after."

"I reckon . . ." Chad paused and then went on. "I reckon Josiah don't think no more of Traitor than we do."

"No, he don't," Amos answered. "Traitor ain't never been anything but mean and ornery, and he ain't never treated his own flesh and blood any different from what he's treated other folks. There's no love lost between Traitor and 'Siah."

It must be awful to think your own father hated you, Chad thought. And worse to think you hated him. He was glad it hadn't happened to him.

"But even if I hadn't knowed about Josiah," Amos went on, "I wouldn't have stood for them being put out of the fort. It's a heap better to shelter the wrong folks than push innocent ones out for the Injuns to git. The Logans ain't never done nothing wrong against Cumberland folks as far as I know. And here in the fort it's easy enough to keep an eye on a woman and two skinny chaps. I don't know to save me why everybody got so roused up about the Logans."

"Me neither," Chad agreed.

"You been good to Josiah," Amos told him. "All you Rabuns been good to the Logans. I reckon they think a heap of that. And I do too. Your pappy's always been a good man."

"But I ain't been," Chad said miserably. "I was bad as the others. I wanted to put the Logans out when we heared Traitor was leading the Injuns. I figgered Josiah was a traitor, too."

"Naw, you didn't neither. You was just mad on account of doing without some of your food," Amos pointed out. "And them other boys acting hateful didn't help none."

He poked Chad in the ribs. "But who was it hollered, and fit so, when the others tried to put Josiah out the gate? No, your heart's in the right place. You wouldn't be your pa's boy if'n that wasn't so."

Chad didn't say any more. Maybe his heart was in the right place, but where had his head been? It shamed him to think he hadn't used his head and thought things through. Even when it had been laid out for him so plain, how it wasn't fair for a boy to get the blame for what his father did, it had taken him a long spell to see it.

Amos took out a piece of leather and a thong and began to mend a torn place in his shirt. Chad

watched, half-asleep, thinking it was kind of foolish of Amos to put a patch on a patch.

The Indian down at the spring commenced to yell again. Chad jumped, and Amos sprang to a loophole.

"Now that's one Injun me and Squencher feel powerful strong about," exclaimed Amos. "And

if'n I put in a double load of powder, I believe I can get him, for a fact," he added.

He fired his rifle into the wall. "Pick that lead out of there for me, Chad," he said. He poured out an extra lot of powder, took a patch, and then rammed a lead ball home. Shoving the rifle through a loophole, he talked, half to himself. "It'd be best if I was to aim just the least mite high, I reckon."

Chad watched through the gun slit beside him. The Indian was filling his kettle again. He lifted it high, letting the water run out slowly. Chad could hardly stand the sight.

Then Squencher spoke out, loud and strong. The Indian dropped the pot, grabbed his shoulder, and sat down suddenly in the spring. The men in the fort whooped and hurrahed. Another brave ran out of the bushes and dragged the wounded Indian out of the water and away.

Chad grinned. "Old Squencher squenched him, for a fact."

Amos nodded. "You run along now and tell Colonel Boyd to step up here. I got a word to say to him in private."

Chad scrambled down the ladder and ran outside. Colonel Boyd was asleep in the shadow of the blockhouse. His mouth was open, and he was snoring. Chad shook him. The Colonel opened his eyes.

"Amos wants to see you up in the blockhouse," the boy told him.

Colonel Boyd stared around with bloodshot eyes, not seeming to hear. He looked like an old, old man. Chad could see his Adam's apple go up and down as he tried to swallow. When he spoke, his voice was dry and scratchy.

"Amos? In the blockhouse?" he repeated.

He sat up and rubbed his eyes till Chad reckoned there was nothing left of them. Then he licked his lips and tried to swallow again. Finally he got to his feet and walked stiffly off. Chad almost felt sorry for him. Maybe being so cocky and puffed up made you thirstier than other folks.

Chad found his family all awake and stirring. He pushed Brose off his quilt and went to sleep almost at once. He awoke later, sitting up with a start. Sarah was screaming, "Fire! Fire! The fort's afire!"

Chapter Ten

The sky was full of fire, long blazing streamers of it. Flaming arrows! Chad scrambled out of his quilt. A shower of sparks drifted down over him, and he beat them away with his hands. They were going to be roasted like a bear haunch! They didn't have a chance without any water. They didn't have the thinnest chance!

Now the arrows were gone, and for the space of a breath the fort was in darkness again. And then a little snake of fire broke out in the dry grass by the gate. A horse screamed and a rifle shot sounded from inside the blockhouse.

Sarah began to yell again. "Fire! We're on fire!"

"Hush, Sarah, hush!" cried Mr. Rabun sharply. "And hand me that deerskin poke."

"It's got meal in it," wailed Sarah, tugging to pull it from under the other bundles.

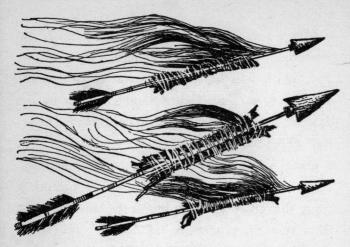

"Hand it here," Mr. Rabun repeated. "If'n we don't git this fire out quick, meal ain't going to be no more use to us than a stick horse."

Sarah dragged the deerskin bag to her father, who snatched it up. Mr. Rabun ran to the burning grass and emptied the meal over it. He beat out the last of the sparks with the empty sack. The smell of scorched corn rose strong on the night air. And now all over the fort folks were yelling and trying to put out little fires.

Mr. Rabun came back and ripped open the deerskin poke. He handed it to Josiah, along with his tomahawk. "You watch for fires, Josiah," he said. "And don't be afraid to chop out any part of the fence that's burning and you can't get to with the deerskin."

Mr. Rabun picked up his rifle. "Chad, get your shooting gear," he told him. "Me and you and Josiah will be along the wall between here and the gate. Tom Caldwell and his pappy are down toward the corner, so we got this side pretty well defended."

Chad slipped the straps over his shoulder. There were three rifle shots in quick succession from the other side of the fort. He wondered what they were shooting at, for it wasn't light enough to see anything, it seemed to him.

"Sarah, you stay with Mammy and take care of Ambrose and the other little ones," Mr. Rabun went on. "Come on, Chad, me and you'll get to a loophole."

Chad and Josiah followed him off and around the dark restless shapes of the horses. "I wish there'd been a time we could of let the horses loose," he said. "If there's fire, them horses are going to be a heap of trouble."

"Is Amos gone?" Chad asked the boy beside him.

"Left as soon as it got dark," Josiah answered.

"Went over the fence so nobody wouldn't hear the gate open."

Chad felt along the wall till he found a low loophole. How far had Amos got by now, he asked himself. Had he got by the savages, ringed around the fort? How many hours would it take to reach help and get back?

He looked out at the night. "What am I supposed to be shooting at?" he asked. "I can't see a frazzling thing."

"Nothing," Mr. Rabun told him. "You're supposed to be watching and listening mostly. We don't want some brave slipping along the wall here, aiming to pile brush against the logs or something like that."

Chad knew about that, how Indians piled grass and sticks against fort walls and then kindled them. That way it was powerful hard for the white folks to reach the blaze without getting shot, and sometimes the fire made a breach in the walls before it could be put out.

But just let these Chickamaugas try it. He gripped his musket hard. Let some brave make a good target of himself, running up here with a lighted torch to kindle the brush. He'd never been in a night skirmish, but his pappy could count on him not to get flustered. It was just that he was so dry, he might go up like gunpowder if one of those arrows came near him.

"Amos says an Injun has to be mighty desperate to use brush and torches," Josiah told them. "And they won't use 'em till they've tried everything else first."

Mr. Rabun agreed that was so.

Out of the darkness there was another rain of blazing arrows. Against the deep night sky they rose in fiery curves and dropped toward the stockade. One stuck in a stump just past Chad. He got to it before Josiah did.

"Why, it ain't nothing but a plain old arrow with some hickory bark tied around it," he said to Josiah, beating out the last ember.

"Well, it works, don't it?" Josiah said impatiently. "You get on back to your loophole. It's my place to put out fires."

Again the arrows fell. This time the roof of the blockhouse caught in several places. The flames spread over the shingles and mounted up the slanting roof with a roar. Somebody inside the upper story began knocking the burning shingles loose with a rifle barrel. They fell in a trail of sparks and lay smoldering on the ground.

For a minute it was bright enough to pick up a pin, and Chad watched the two oldest Adair girls loading rifles for Mr. Adair and Colonel Boyd. It made for fast firing, for no sooner did the men shoot one rifle than the girls handed them another, all ready to fire. He was glad no girl was loading for him. He'd a heap rather do his own. But it seemed a shame for Colonel Boyd to have two rifles and Josiah to have none.

"Maybe all the fighting is going to be on that side," he thought, and he didn't know whether he was glad or sorry.

Before he turned back to his loophole, Chad saw a man climb a little way up the side of the blockhouse and knock down an arrow stuck in one of the logs. Most of the roof of the blockhouse was gone. "I reckon that's the best way there is to keep your roof from catching fire, not to have one," Chad thought.

"Mr. Rabun," said Josiah suddenly. "Most all them logs between you and Chad is doty. I seen 'em this afternoon. They're most nigh rotted through near the ground."

Mr. Rabun bent to touch a few of the logs. He whistled softly. "Dang!" he exclaimed. "Well, there ain't nothing we can do about it now. You'll just have to watch close. Any little spark'll set 'em afire, they're so dry. And Chad, you get back to that loophole."

Chad went back and looked down the slope toward the pitch black emptiness at the bottom. There was not a spark, not a moving shadow there. He'd almost rather be over on the other wall where the fighting was going on than here, staring at the darkness till white spots dazzled in front of his eyes, and waiting, waiting.

What few dogs hadn't run off were right outside, howling their fool heads off. He wished they'd shut up. They made him jumpy. He was bone-tired in spite of his sleep, and the smoke from fires and gunpowder stung his cracked, dry lips and tongue.

"Rabun! Mr. Rabun!" somebody yelled, and Chad jerked his head around to see. It was Gil McKaye, limping toward them. "Colonel Boyd says you and Caldwell get over there. The Injuns has got a heap of brush piled against the fence, and they're trying to set a torch to it. We can't hardly keep 'em off."

Chad's heart leaped in his chest. The Chickamaugas must be pretty desperate then, according to what Josiah had told them. This would be their big try. He gripped his musket, scared. Suppose the men couldn't keep the warriors off? What in creation would happen to them, shut up in a fort with the walls so rotted they were apt to blaze up quick as punk wood and with no springs and no well, with not even so much as a gourdful of milk to pour on a fire?

He watched his father and Mr. Caldwell run off. Now only three boys and a man with a bad wounded leg were left on that part of the palisade. "I just hope the Injuns don't know it," thought Chad, putting his face to the loophole again. It was queer how black and still and peaceful it was outside and how awful it was in the fort with flames leaping up here and there and men shouting and guns going off and the horses stamping and screaming. He almost wished he was outside.

Three fiery arrows climbed up the slope toward him. He fired quickly at the spot where the arrows seemed to come from, but he knew it was out of range for his musket. Gil shot, too, but there was no way to tell if he'd hit his target.

Two of the arrows fell inside the station. Chad could hear Josiah beating at them with the deerskin. But the third fell outside. Chad craned and peered to see where it went.

"It must of gone out," called Gil. "I can't see no sign of it."

Chad didn't answer. He strained to hear what was happening on the north side. Had they held the Indians off? He leaned against the fence, tired and lightheaded. He reckoned he must have a fever, his head was so hot and his arms, too. Even the wall seemed to burn him, right through his shirt. He looked down then and saw the little tongue of flame licking around the logs and the smoke twisting up like a grapevine.

"Gil!" he bawled. "Josiah! The fence here's on fire—on the outside!"

Josiah came toward him, dragging the skin. Gil limped painfully up beside him. "Great day in the morning!" Gil swore. "Josiah, run get one of them muddy deerskins at the spring. And tell the Colonel we need help bad!"

Josiah dropped the hatchet and ran.

"Looky yonder!" groaned Chad. "Up there near the top. This here whole log's afire, Gil."

"We'll have to chop it out afore it catches the other logs," Gil cried. "Quick! Hand me that ax."

Gil took it and began to cut away at the pole. Chad couldn't believe it would take so long to chop down one log. "Hurry up, Gil!"

"Take care," called the Colonel. "Take care! I'm a-coming."

The blazing log fell inside the fort. The Colonel had to hop to get out of the way. "Roll it over yonder," gasped Gil, leaning against the fence, wiping the sweat from his face.

Josiah and Tom shoved it toward the center of the fort.

"Them next two will have to come out," Chad yelled. "They've caught good."

"Naw, naw," the Colonel croaked hoarsely. "It'll make too big a gap." He put his head and shoulders through the gap in the wall, flailing at the burning logs with the muddy deerskin. Two shots smashed into the fence, but the Colonel didn't seem to know.

"Here," panted Gil, handing Chad the ax. "I can't do no more. You chop awhile. The Colonel ain't doing nothing but fanning that fire."

He leaned against the wall and shouted, "Get away from there, Colonel Boyd, and let Chad chop out them logs. We can't save 'em."

Chad ran at the fence. A third pole was already smoking. Another moment and it would flare up. "Watch out, Colonel," he yelled.

Colonel Boyd drew his head part way in, looking bewildered. The log beside him flamed, and smoke billowed over him.

Chad swung the hatchet, whanged down with all his strength, and the pole cracked and swayed. "Watch out," screamed Chad, jumping back.

The picket fell, smacking the ground with a great wave of sparks and flames as the rotten wood scattered from the impact. Chad threw his arm over his face, and when he looked again, he saw the Colonel stagger blindly toward him with his hair and his wool hat and his shirt in flames.

Chapter Eleven

Chad screamed in horror. He ran at the Colonel and began to beat at the flames with his hands. He pulled off the hat and flung it to the ground. He stripped a big piece of the burning shirt from the man's back, and it curled around his hands, searing them back and front. He shook it off frantically and slapped at the Colonel's clothes again.

Gil McKaye shoved him aside and wrapped a deerskin around Colonel Boyd's shoulders, smothering the last of the flames. The Colonel sank to the ground, moaning. His hair was singed almost off. Big blisters were already forming on his back and shoulders.

Chad stared at him stupidly, holding his scorched hands out in front of him. The pain came throbbing up his arms till for a minute he thought he might yell out. His mammy came running up and took his arm, but Chad jerked away from her.

"The fence!" he shouted. "Somebody's got to see to the fence."

"Somebody'll look after it," his mammy reassured him, edging him gently away.

Mrs. Boyd pushed past them and stooped over her husband. "He's a-going to die," she sobbed. "He was sick anyway, had a fever. Oh, I begged him to stay in the blockhouse. He's so stubborn." She sat down beside him and covered her face with her hands. "He'll die, I know in reason he will," she wept.

Mrs. Adair was on her knees examining the burns. "No, he ain't neither," she said. "We'll get some grease on them blisters, and he'll be all right. Them burns ain't deep. Now don't take on so. There ain't no need to cry."

Mrs. Boyd went on talking and crying.

"Chad, I'll just doctor you first off," Mrs. Rabun told him. "Mrs. Adair'll need help tending to the Boyds. I reckon they'll both need nursing."

Chad hardly heard her. His hands ached and stung up to his elbows. He was in a kind of daze of pain and terror. He walked with his mammy, but his feet kept wobbling and stumbling under him.

"Sit down here away from the young 'uns," his mammy told him. "You don't want them around."

She brought some bear grease and smoothed it gently over the backs of his hands and across the palms. Then she wound some strips of cloth around his hands loosely. "There ain't much use bandaging a burn, for a fact. It's more to keep you from breaking them blisters than anything," she said. "I can't do nothing else for you. You try to get some sleep, you hear?"

She went away, and Chad sat there with his hands held stiffly in front of him. He couldn't very well get to sleep with his fingers feeling like somebody was trying to take the skin off them with a dull knife. Oh, he wished he had some water. He'd give a year off his life and throw in his musket too for a noggin of water, any kind of water.

There was hardly any firing now. The fires were out, and he couldn't see anything. But he reckoned they must have whipped the Indians again. He wondered if any more of the fence had been burned. Well, it probably wouldn't be as big a hole as he had chopped, a hole big enough to let all the Chickamauga tribe in.

He moved about uneasily. Maybe the warriors were out there right now, waiting till the settlers quieted before rushing through the hole. Oh, he wished morning would come. He wished Amos would hurry back. He wished—he kicked out savagely at nothing. There wasn't any use wishing. Wishing never saved a body from the Indians as far as he knew.

He could hear the Colonel groaning through the dark. Once he hollered out something about shooting redskins.

Somebody was walking toward him. "That you, Chad?" his father asked. "You bad off?"

"Not too bad off," Chad answered.

Mr. Rabun leaned over and touched his bandaged hands. "If'n I'd come over last month when I made out to do it, I'd of got them logs out of there," he went on. "I knowed Amos was gone off and couldn't look after things proper. But I never got here. If'n I had, this wouldn't of happened."

"Did you drive off the redskins?" asked Chad. There wasn't any more use talking about "If'n I had" than there was wishing.

"We sure did that," Mr. Rabun answered more cheerfully. "We gave 'em what for with the chill off. They must have lost fifteen braves burning the fence on the north side. But they made a good-sized gap there too."

He yawned. "I aim to get some sleep," he said wearily. "We got to keep watch the rest of the night, and it'll be my turn 'way before I'm ready for it."

Chad lay down, and the pain in his hands made him grit his teeth. His hands felt big as piggins. He tried shifting them here and there, but it did no good. He sat up again, wincing at the sharp stabbing in his hands. Finally his mammy came back. She had Josiah with her.

"Don't you want to lay down, Chad?" she asked.

"No, ma'm, I couldn't sleep noway," he told her. "How's the Colonel?"

"He's right bad off," she answered. "He keeps asking for water, and I reckon he needs it, though I'd say a good hot tea would be better for him."

"Can't you hear him groaning and begging?" asked Josiah. "I can't hardly stand listening to him."

"The old feller's most out of his head," Mrs. Rabun said. "He can't help hollering out."

"I know he can't," Josiah told her. "But I don't like to hear it, just the same."

Chad didn't like hearing it either, and he liked it even less as the night wore slowly away. Not many folks slept. They moved around in the dark, stumbling over each other, trying to forget how weary and thirsty they were, trying to get away from the pitiful sound of Colonel Boyd's voice pleading for water.

"Maybe it'll rain," Josiah said once.

"Maybe so," Chad answered. But it wouldn't. The dim haze over the stars was from the heat and dust. It couldn't possibly be rain clouds.

Chad dozed off, and when he woke, he could hear voices near. Mr. Renfro was saying they ought to give up. "By daylight the redskins can see how bad off we be. They'll come right on in through that big gap in the north wall or this here hole near the gate. We ought to parley with

Traitor right now, give up and be prisoners. It might save our scalps and get us water."

His voice was slow and heavy. The very sound of it made a body feel discouraged and sad. Chad wished he wouldn't talk so. Folks were hard pressed enough now to keep up their spirits. Mr. Renfro ought to keep his sad thoughts to himself. Besides, Amos was bringing help. He'd be here in a few hours with men from the Bluffs.

Leastways, Chad hoped Amos would make it. There was a heap of things that could happen to a man between here and the Bluffs.

"Now, there ain't no sense in me thinking that way," he said to himself. He was nigh as bad as Mr. Renfro. But he'd keep his mouth shut on his doubts and fears anyway.

He sat up, working his dry tongue around in his mouth until he could speak. "Josiah," he whispered.

"I'm over here," Josiah answered. "Do your hands hurt a heap?"

"No. They ain't so bad as they was," Chad told him. "How come you ain't asleep?"

"I been asleep some," Josiah said. "It's mostly

157

the Colonel keeps me awake. I wisht there was some way to ease him."

Chad could hear the Colonel. He moaned and wailed out; his voice went up and down like a screech owl's. Then he screamed hoarsely, "Oh, don't hold me! I just aim to git a little water. Just a gourdful."

Chad shivered. He wished he hadn't been the one to swing the ax and bring the rotten logs down on Colonel Boyd. In his mind he could see the Colonel, plain as day, standing there with his hair ablaze and flames running up his arms and shoulders.

"How long till daylight, you reckon?" Chad asked the other.

"I wouldn't know," Josiah answered. "But I reckon I ain't going to be able to sit still here no longer." He got to his feet.

Chad was tired. But he didn't want to stay here by himself, listening to the Colonel and waiting for his hands to start hurting worse. "Wait a minute," he said. "I'll go with you."

They moved off along the fence in the dark, careful to go around the dark figures stretched out on the ground. They came to the gap near the gate, and Chad could smell the charred wood. Some logs had been stuck upright in the breach.

"Reckon where them logs come from?" Chad asked Josiah.

"I heard Mr. Caldwell say he aimed to use the roof poles from the top of the blockhouse," Josiah answered.

"Well, they ain't doing a heap of good like this," Chad said. "They're put in the ground so loose, they're already leaning every whichaway. Anybody could come in." He stuck his head between the logs and snatched it back. His heart was pounding so he could hardly breathe.

"There's somebody outside there," he whispered. "Somebody standing right there close to the fence."

There was not a sound from outside. Finally Josiah poked his head through. "Who's there?" he asked softly. "Who is it?"

"Who does he figger it is?" Chad asked himself. "Traitor? Or does he reckon any Injun would be fool enough to speak out?"

Chad was surprised when an answer came. "It's me, Anna Boyd," a voice said. "I just come out. I'm a-going to fetch some water."

"You hadn't ought to go," said Josiah after a minute. "The Injuns'll git you. They're bound to hear you at the spring."

"I'm a-going," said Mrs. Boyd firmly. "My man's been crying for water this livelong night and hasn't none of them growed men said they'd fetch him so much as a nogginful. I've begged and begged, asked 'em please to get some water, till I done well-nigh wore out my voice. So now I'm going to fetch Abijah some spring water afore he dies for lack of it."

Chad didn't know what to do. He couldn't grab her with his burned hands, and Josiah'd never hold her by himself. Maybe he'd best run for his pappy.

"You got something to fetch water in?" asked Josiah.

"I got a piggin," Mrs. Boyd answered. She held it up, and it knocked against the fence.

Quick as light, Josiah reached out and grabbed it. "I'll go for you," he said and scrambled through the logs and disappeared.

"He'll git killed," Chad gasped. The Indians would get him. There'd be Indians at the spring,

he knew in reason. He turned and ran. His pappy wouldn't let Josiah go and get killed.

"Pappy!" he cried. "Pappy!"

Somebody seized him by the shoulder. "Hush, boy, hush."

"Where's my pappy?" asked Chad. "Where's Henry Rabun?"

"Chad, what ails you?" his pappy asked. "This here *is* me."

"At the hole," Chad panted. "Mrs. Boyd was a-going for water, and Josiah went for her. Don't let him get shot, Pappy."

People hollered to know what was going on. "Is it the Injuns?" cried Mrs. Adair.

"We'd best give up and save our lives," shouted Mr. Renfro.

"What is it, Rabun, what is it?" bawled William Bennett.

"How can I find out with all this racket?" Mr. Rabun cried. "Hush a minute. Now, Chad, where's Mrs. Boyd?"

"She's . . ." began Chad.

"I'm right here," she answered. She had got back inside the fence. "I don't know what all the fuss is about. I was aiming to get Abijah some water, and some lad went for me."

"Who was it?" asked Mr. Caldwell. "It warn't Tom!"

"Naw, it wasn't," snapped Chad. "It was Josiah Logan."

"Well, whoever 'twas, he's a fine brave lad," said Mrs. Boyd. "Worth any three of you men. Any one of you could of got down there in the dark if you hadn't been so spineless."

"Now, Mrs. Boyd," spoke up Mr. Adair. "That ain't hardly fair. It would of been certain death to go down there."

"The boy went," said Mrs. Boyd simply.

"Likely he didn't go to get water for you," Mr. Stonecipher said. "Likely he just took this chance to slip away to his father."

"He didn't neither," cried Chad. "His pappy don't like him, and he don't care for his pappy. Amos said so."

"Stonecipher, I don't know how come you to talk like that," Mr. Rabun said. "Josiah could of run off anytime if'n he wanted to get back to his pappy. He ain't done one thing to make you think he was a bad one."

"That's right," said Gil McKaye suddenly. "He toted his end of the log like a good 'un this night. I'll 'low he's a true fighter."

"Ain't we said so all along?" asked Chad. "Ain't Amos said so? But that ain't helping Josiah none now. Pappy, can't you go help him?"

"No, Chad, I'd do him more good staying right here," Mr. Rabun told him. "Two might make a heap of noise. By hisself, Josiah's got a chance to slip down there and back safely."

"If he comes back," some woman added.

There was a silence. Then Mr. Adair spoke. "Well, Rabun, if the boy has run off, we won't fault you none. You ain't to blame. If'n he brings back the water, then I'll take your word for it, he's all right. But I reckon he ain't coming back."

"Give him time," said Gil McKaye.

"He's got all the time 'twixt now and daylight," said Mr. Stonecipher.

"He never sounded like he was running off," said Mrs. Boyd. "I look for him back."

Chad rushed back to the fence, pushing his face between the logs. What was that? Did he hear somebody yell? No, it must have been a bird. He strained his eyes to see a shadow, his ears to hear the sound of water sloshing in the piggin.

But if he could hear it, the Indians could hear it too. Would they spring out of the woods and cut Josiah down with a tomahawk? Or worse, take him prisoner? Maybe Traitor could save him. Chad reckoned not; Traitor was all Indian.

"Water!" came the Colonel's thick voice.

Josiah was brave. "I couldn't of done it," thought Chad. "I couldn't of crept down that hill in the dark, with every bush liable to turn out to be an Injun. And I reckon Mr. Adair and Mr. Stonecipher ain't so brave as that either."

But why didn't Josiah come back? What had happened? Could the Indians have killed him as silently as they had killed Walter Stonecipher? Chad could see off in the woods a gleaming shape that was the big white trunk of a button tree. Oh, don't let Josiah be dead, he prayed.

He wondered where Mrs. Logan was. Did she know Josiah was out there in the dark? He hoped she was asleep. He hoped she didn't know they were all waiting here for Josiah to get killed.

It was so still and black. The minutes went by, and Chad couldn't hear anything but the sound of his own heart thudding and Tom Caldwell running his thumbnail up and down his leather breeches.

"Well, I'm satisfied he ain't coming back," said Mr. Stonecipher loudly.

And just then Chad saw it, the shadow creeping up to the wall. For a minute he almost busted open with pride in Josiah, who had gone alone to fetch water for the man who had tried to put him out of the fort and who had made the perilous trip down the hill and back with the Indians all around him.

"Here he comes," Chad called out softly. "He's almost here!"

Josiah reached the fence and held out the piggin. "I spilled a heap of it coming up," he said sadly. "I'm sorry as can be."

Chapter Twelve

"Don't drink a heap now," said Mrs. Rabun, holding a gourd for Chad to drink. "Just a little swaller or so and then you can have some more in a spell."

Chad rolled the water around in his mouth. His tongue was still dry and leathery. But oh, how wonderful the water felt sliding down his throat.

He looked around and saw Billy Renfro and Tom Caldwell kneeling by the spring pouring water on each other's heads. Tom had already been sick once from drinking too much water after such a long time without. Chad was almost glad his hands were bandaged. If they hadn't been, he might have run to the spring like Tom and flung himself down to drink spring water by the gallon. And then he'd have been sick along with Tom.

He drew a deep breath. "Ain't it a fine day?"

he asked his mammy. "The sky's so blue and them maples so red. I'm in such good heart I could most nigh sprout wings and fly."

His mammy laughed. "If'n it had been raining, snowing, or earthquaking, I reckon I would of thought it was a fine pretty day when I heared

Amos and them whooping in the woods this morning."

Chad grinned. "Did you see Gil McKaye? He did a one-legged dance, waving his mammy's best quilt like he didn't have good sense."

"Poor Mrs. Adair," said Mrs. Rabun. "She laughed and she cried till we had to burn feathers under her nose to quiet her."

"I tell you what was the worst part of it all," said Chad soberly. "It was all that long time after

Josiah brung the water, whilst we was a-waiting for Amos. Hearing the Colonel drink water like to of drove me plumb out of my mind. And then I got to thinking, 'Suppose help ain't coming.' It was the worst waiting ever I done."

"You can have a swaller more now," Mrs. Rabun said, raising the gourd. "The Colonel's a heap better. He'll have to stay here at the station for a spell, but he'll be all right."

Chad drank again. Over the edge of the dipper he could see the fort gate standing open and folks going in and out, talking and laughing like they were at a play party. It was sweet as the taste of clear water to be outside those log walls and know the Indians were gone, gone back to their towns in Chickamauga country.

And it was better yet to have folks friendly together. Mrs. Logan was sitting on a log talking with Mrs. Stonecipher. The oldest Adair girl was helping Robert Logan drink. But Chad figured Sarah was happiest of all. She was washing the Logan baby!

"Now where's Ambrose got to?" asked Mrs. Rabun suddenly. "I told your pappy to keep an eye on him, but he ain't done it. I'd best go see."

She went off and left Chad standing there feeling foolish with his hands stuck out in front of him. He wished his pappy would hurry up and get through talking so they could start for home. The horses had long since been watered properly and were in good enough shape to travel. There wasn't a heap to take back anyway. The food was all gone, some of the quilts were burned, and one piggin had been busted. They had just theirselves mostly to get home, but that was enough. He didn't even care if they went back to find their cabin burned by the savages.

"You git some water, Chad?" called Mr. Adair. "Lemme fetch you some."

Chad started to shake his head, but then he figured he ought to let Mr. Adair favor him a mite. "I'd be obliged," he said.

And when Mr. Adair brought a nogginful of water, Chad smiled and said, "Thank ye kindly." He took a swallow or two. Mr. Adair wasn't so handy as Mrs. Rabun; a heap of water ran down Chad's chin and inside his shirt. But it didn't matter. Nothing much mattered but standing here knowing the Indians were gone and the fort had held out, and now they were going back home.

"Tastes mighty good, don't it?" Mr. Adair exclaimed. "I reckon there ain't nothing on this green earth so welcome as water when you been dry for a longish spell."

"That's right," Chad agreed. He didn't say anything else. He still felt a little uneasy around Mr. Adair, because of the fight they'd had. It wasn't that he held it against Mr. Adair. It was just, he reckoned, that he never would feel quite the same about anything. These three days in the fort had stretched out half a lifetime.

He'd learned a lot in three days, more than he'd learned in all his years before. He'd learned about hating and being hated. And most important of all he'd truly learned what his pappy meant about thinking things through and why a body had to do it, how nobody ought to be blamed for things somebody else had done.

"Is that enough?" asked Mr. Adair, and Chad nodded. "Much obliged," he said. He walked away and sat on a rock. He was thinking about how Amos had fussed when he came into the fort earlier this morning to say the Indians were gone.

The scout had told the folks in the fort a heap,

about how mean they'd been to the Logans. Mr. Adair had said they were sorry. "We're as sorry as can be," he had said. "But no harm's done."

Amos had turned red. "No harm's done," he cried out, "but it come a heap too close for comfort. I recollect how the redskins come over the fence whilst you was all picking on a pint-sized boy and a poorly woman, folks that never done a mean thing in their lives. We all like to got killed, and I hope it learned you a lesson."

Now everybody was being friendly to the Logans. And most folks were being friendly to Chad. But he wished Tom and David and the rest would be a mite friendlier. He wasn't mad at them any more. He didn't rightly see he had any reason to be.

They were all there by the spring, Abel and David and Tom and Billy, talking to Josiah.

"Be you going to stay at the fort with Amos?" asked Abel.

"Naw," Josiah answered. "My mammy's going to stay, and the least ones, to help nurse Colonel Boyd. But I'm a-going with the Rabuns to help out."

"Come help out with us," said Tom and

laughed. "You can do my share of the chores any time you got a mind to."

"It ain't that I got such a mind to," spoke Josiah carefully. "It's on account of Chad getting his hands burned. And besides the Rabuns has been good to me."

They all turned and looked at Chad. He didn't know what to do exactly, but finally he grinned faintly.

"Now how come I wasn't the one to git my hands burned?" asked Tom sorrowfully. "Looky there, Chad ain't aiming to do a thing for a month, just set around and be waited on."

Billy came up to Chad and lifted one of his bandaged hands. "Ugh, smell the bear grease," he shouted.

"Does it still hurt?" asked Abel, and Chad said, "No, not much."

"How you aim to eat?" asked David.

"Oh, I reckon he'll manage to eat, if'n he has to do it with his toes," said Abel. "You know in reason he ain't fixing to starve, David Stonecipher."

"I can hold a spoon if I can't do nothing else," Chad told them.

Tom sighed. "But you can't tote water or use a chopping ax," he stated. "Ain't you lucky?"

"Well, you could hold your hands in the fire if you're so all-fired anxious to git burned," jeered Abel. "Ain't that right, Chad?"

"Or his mammy could burn him with a switch," giggled Billy. "Now he'll just have to wait till next time we fort up."

"I hope that'll be a long time off," said Chad.

"We didn't get no wrassling done, hardly," complained David. "And now it's too late. I would of beat every one of you, I know."

"Not Josiah, he's stronger than you," pointed out Abel. "He's light, but he's strong."

"Come along, Abel," called Mr. Adair. "We're ready to leave."

"You wait," shouted David as Abel ran toward his waiting family. "Abel, you'll just see I can throw all of you."

"Naw, naw," Chad exclaimed. "I'm the tee-total champeen bear cat when it comes to wrassling."

Josiah winked at Chad, and Chad burst out laughing. He didn't have to worry. They were all friends together.

"Yonder comes Amos," Tom pointed out.

The scout came down the hill swinging his rifle.

"Ain't Amos grand?" admired David. "I wisht my mammy would let me wear leggings and a breechclout."

"Howdy, boys," Amos greeted them. "I heared tell you young 'uns had drunk up every last drop in this spring, and I come to see if it was the truth."

"Naw, we left you some," Tom told him. "Just the least little trickle, though."

Amos laughed. " 'Siah," he said. "I been talking to Mrs. Boyd. She wants to give you something for fetching the water. I said she'd ought to give you a rifle. The Colonel's got two fine ones and money to buy two more, if'n he has the notion. So you take it."

Josiah grinned all over his face. "For a fact, Amos, can I have it?" he cried. "Do you reckon I'd ought to take it?"

Amos laughed. "Go 'long with you. You could of got scalped."

"Was you scared?" asked Billy.

Josiah nodded. "I was scared all right," he admitted. "I reckon the Injuns might of been gone by then, but I didn't know it. And I was shaking, couldn't hardly fill the piggin, I was a-shaking so. And when I lay down and took a gulp for myself, it seemed like you could hear me swallering clean to Kentucky. So I just filled the piggin and come on back."

"I couldn't of done it," said Chad.

"Me neither," added Billy.

"Amos, when can I get the rifle?" asked Josiah.

"Run on up there now," Amos told him.

Josiah skedaddled up the hill. The other boys started off after him. Amos held Chad by the shoulder.

"Chad," he said. "You know that rifle I was getting for Josiah? Well, he don't need it now. who you reckon needs it?"

Chad glanced up quickly at Amos. The scout wasn't even looking at him at all.

"I . . . I don't rightly know," stammered Chad. "Billy nor Abel or none of them have a rifle. Some of 'em ain't even got a musket."

"That's true," nodded Amos. "But I mean for

somebody to have it that really deserves it."

"Well," Chad said slowly. "Gil McKaye, now, he might welcome a fine new gun."

"Is that right?" asked Amos. He rubbed his jaw and grinned at Chad. "Now, there's a young feller I know of needs this rifle. I'm proud to know him. I reckon he's a brave lad and had a sight to put up with these three days. He saved my life, it seems like, and fit like a young painter, and did a heap of good deeds. Held his tongue when he'd like to have shouted out, and stood up for them weaker than hisself. And liked to got his hands burned plumb off putting out a fire."

"Me?" gasped Chad. "You mean me, Amos?" He didn't know what else to say. He was fair flabbergasted.

Amos shook his shoulder gently, grinning down at him. "Who else?" he asked and walked back toward the fort.

VOYAGER BOOKS